P9-DFF-689

NOBODY'S DUCK

Words and pictures by Mary Sullivan

HOUGHTON MIFFLIN HARCOURT
Boston   New York

Haverstraw King's Daughters
Public Library
10 W. Ramapo Road
Garnerville, NY 10923

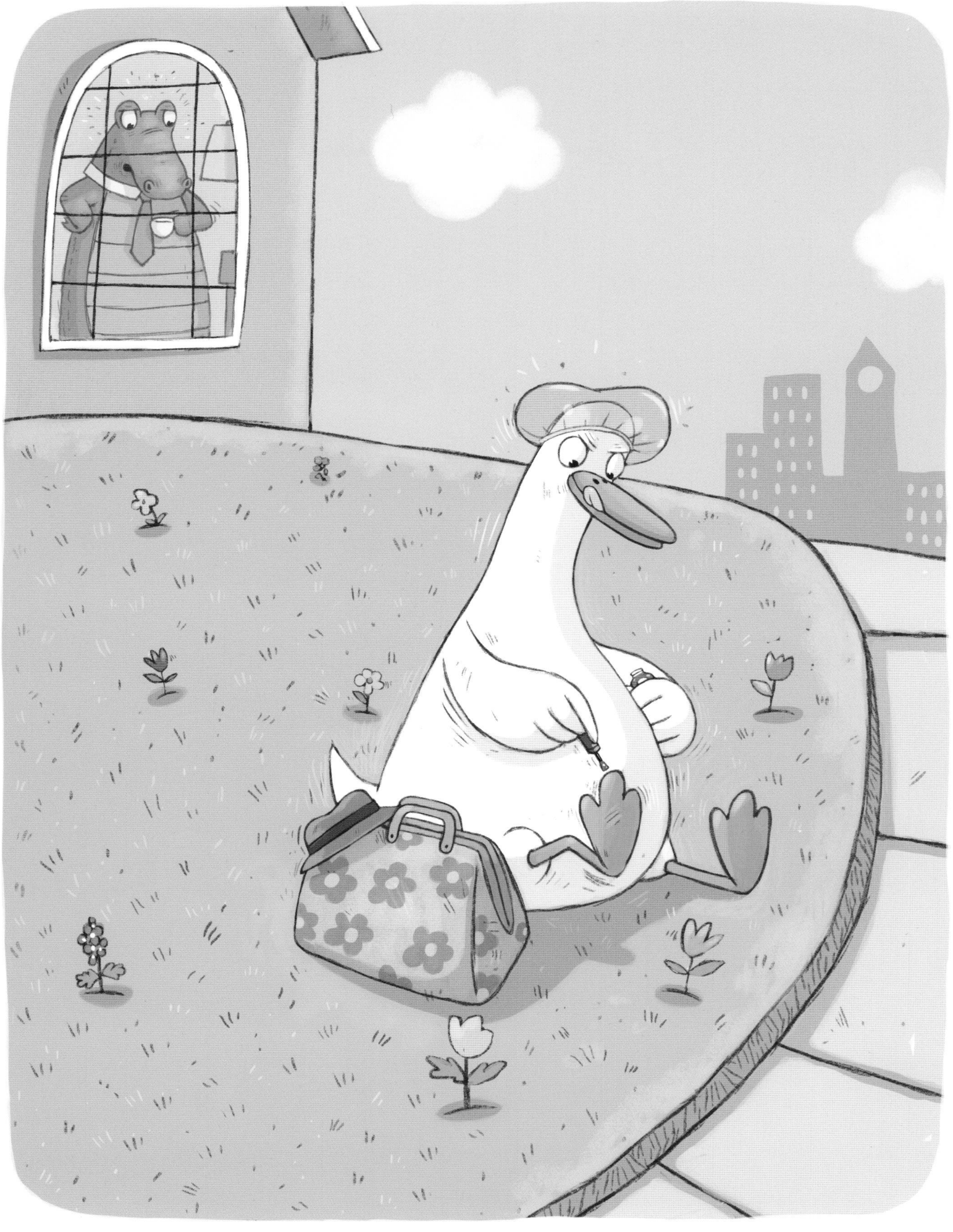

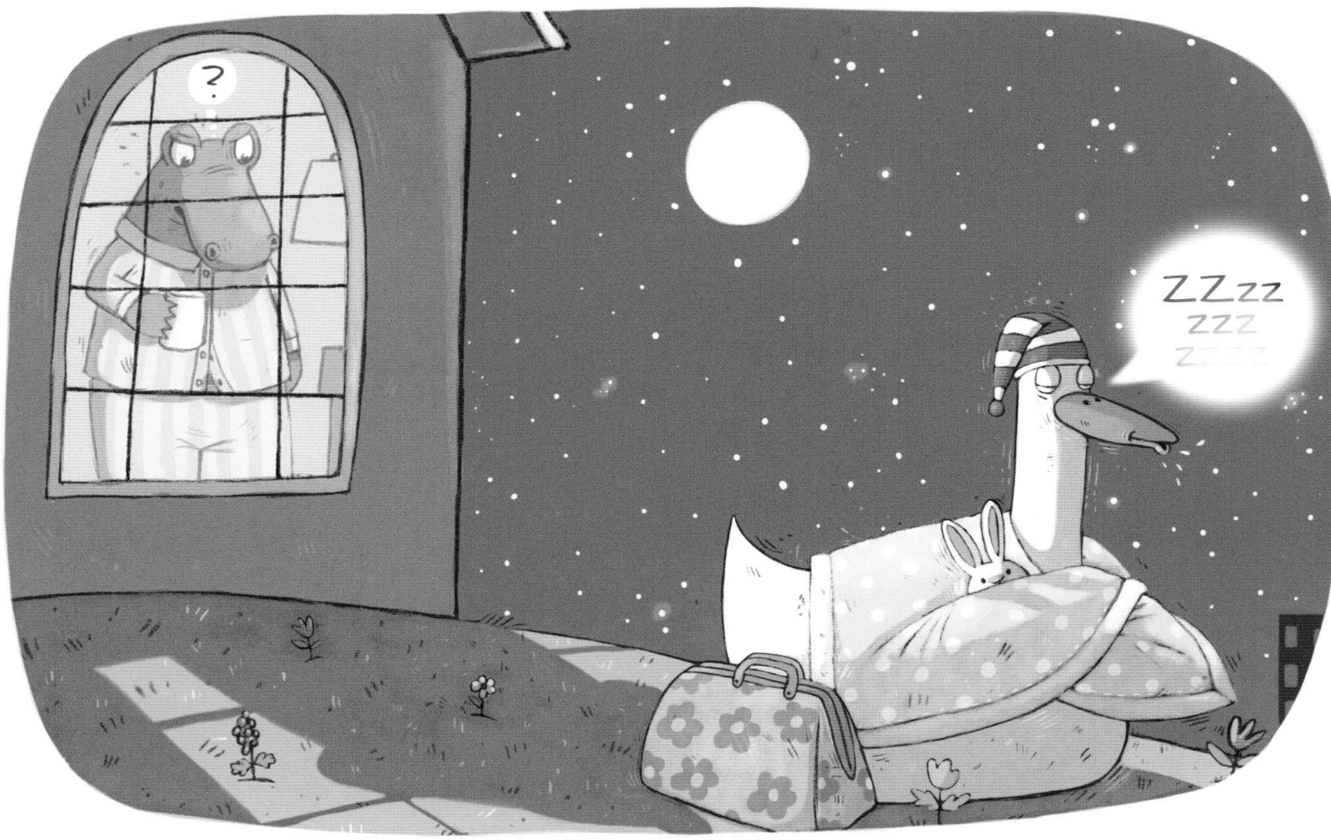
?
ZZzz
zzz
zzzz

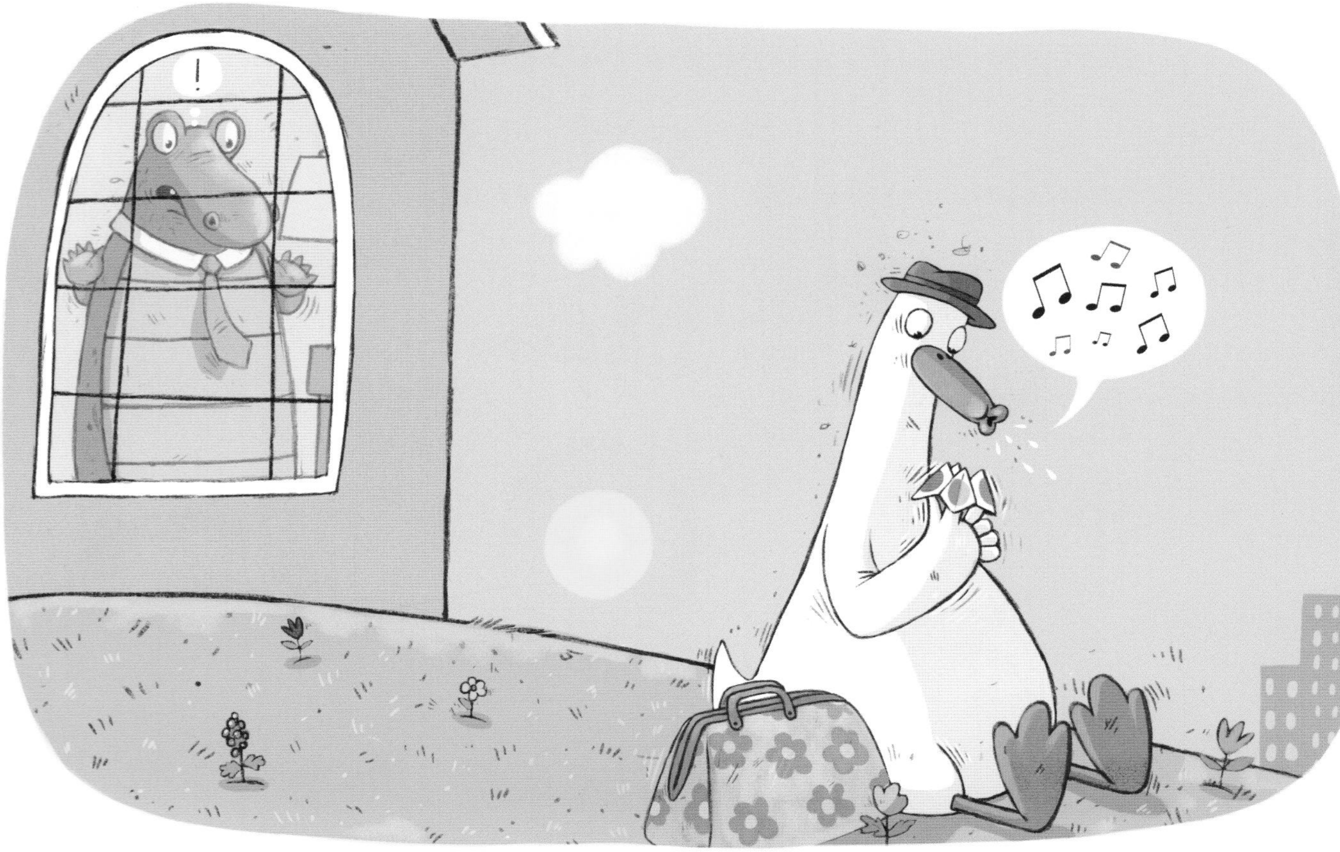
!

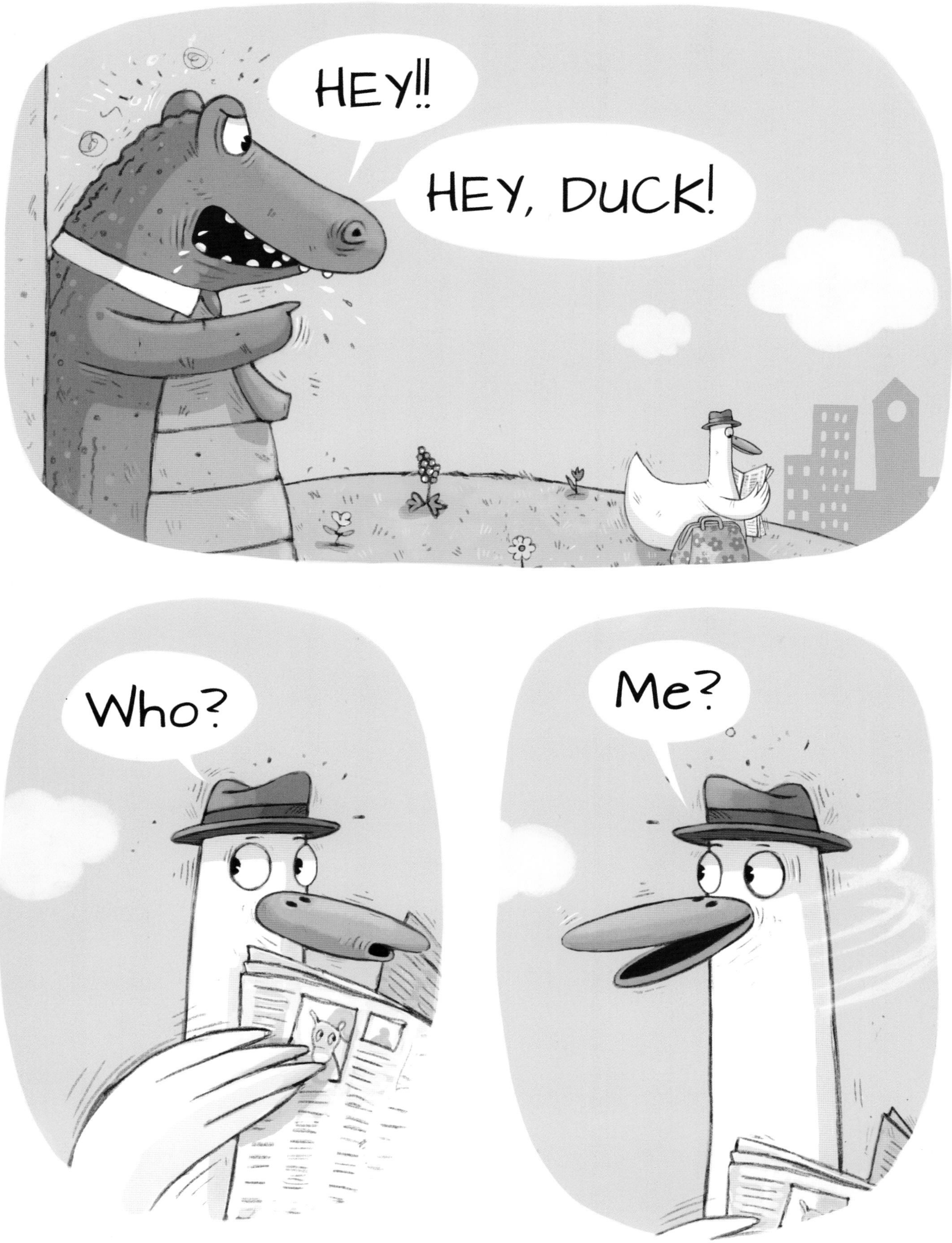
HEY!!
HEY, DUCK!
Who?
Me?

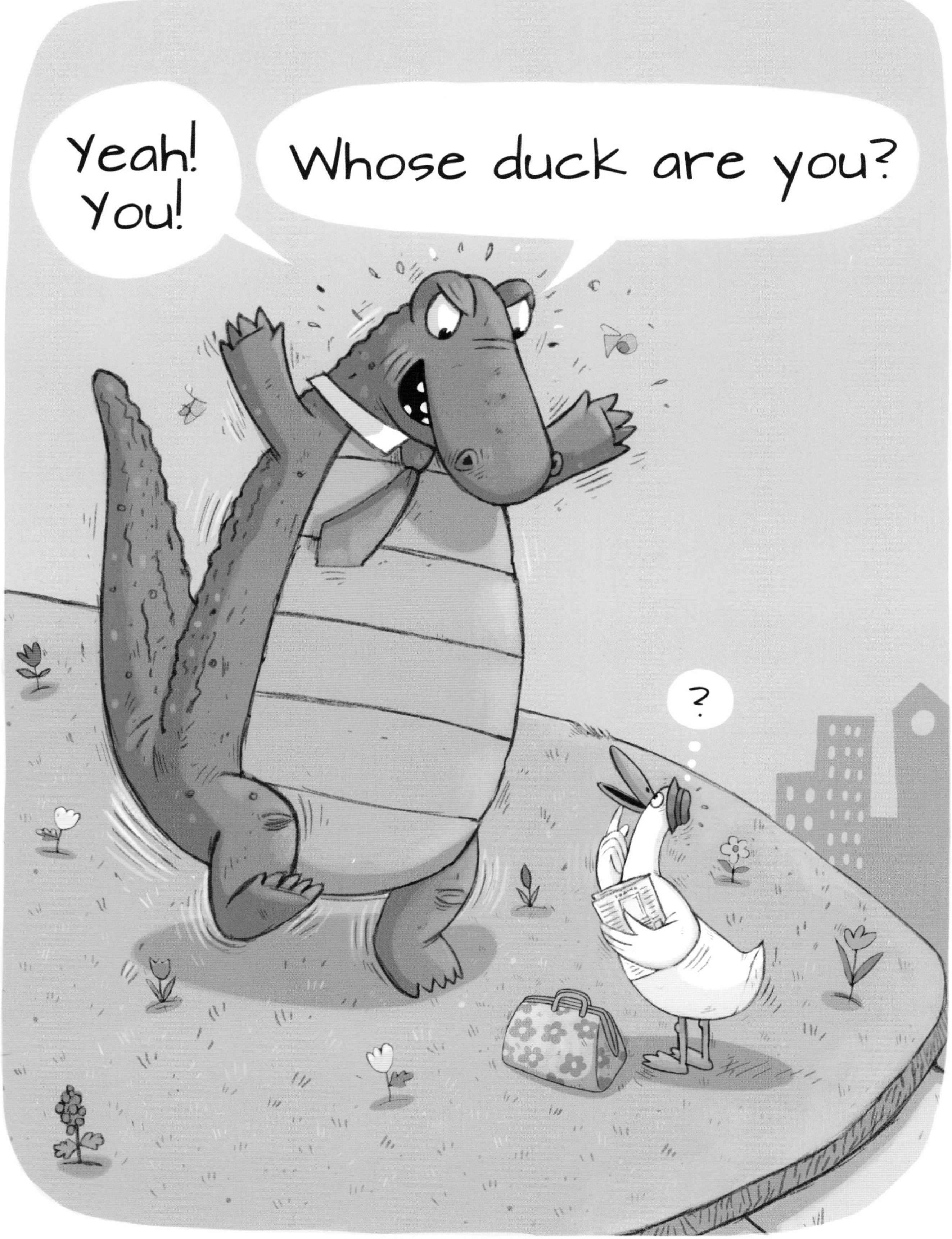
Yeah! You!
Whose duck are you?
?

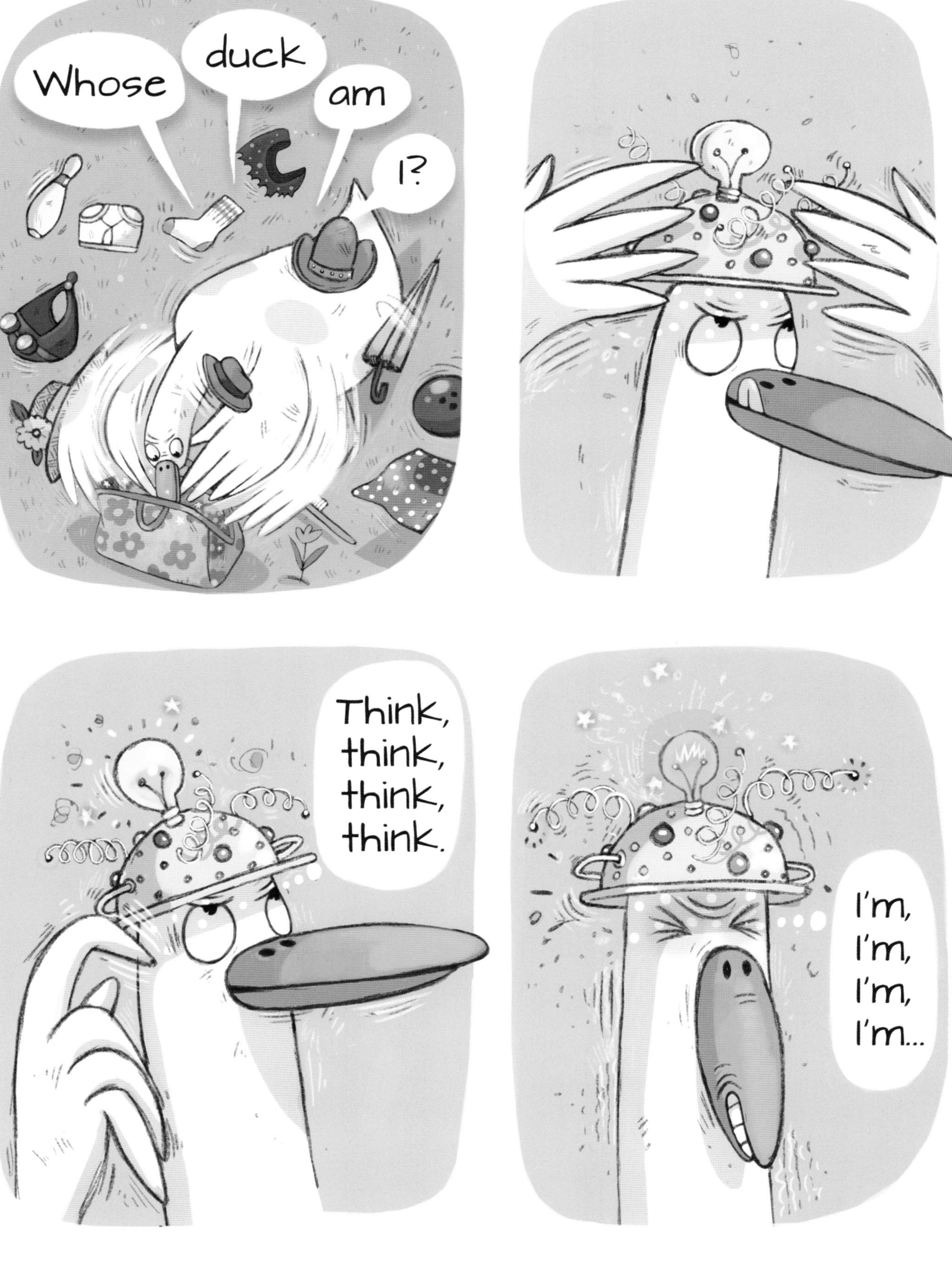
Whose
duck
am
I?
Think,
think,
think,
think.
I'm,
I'm,
I'm,
I'm...

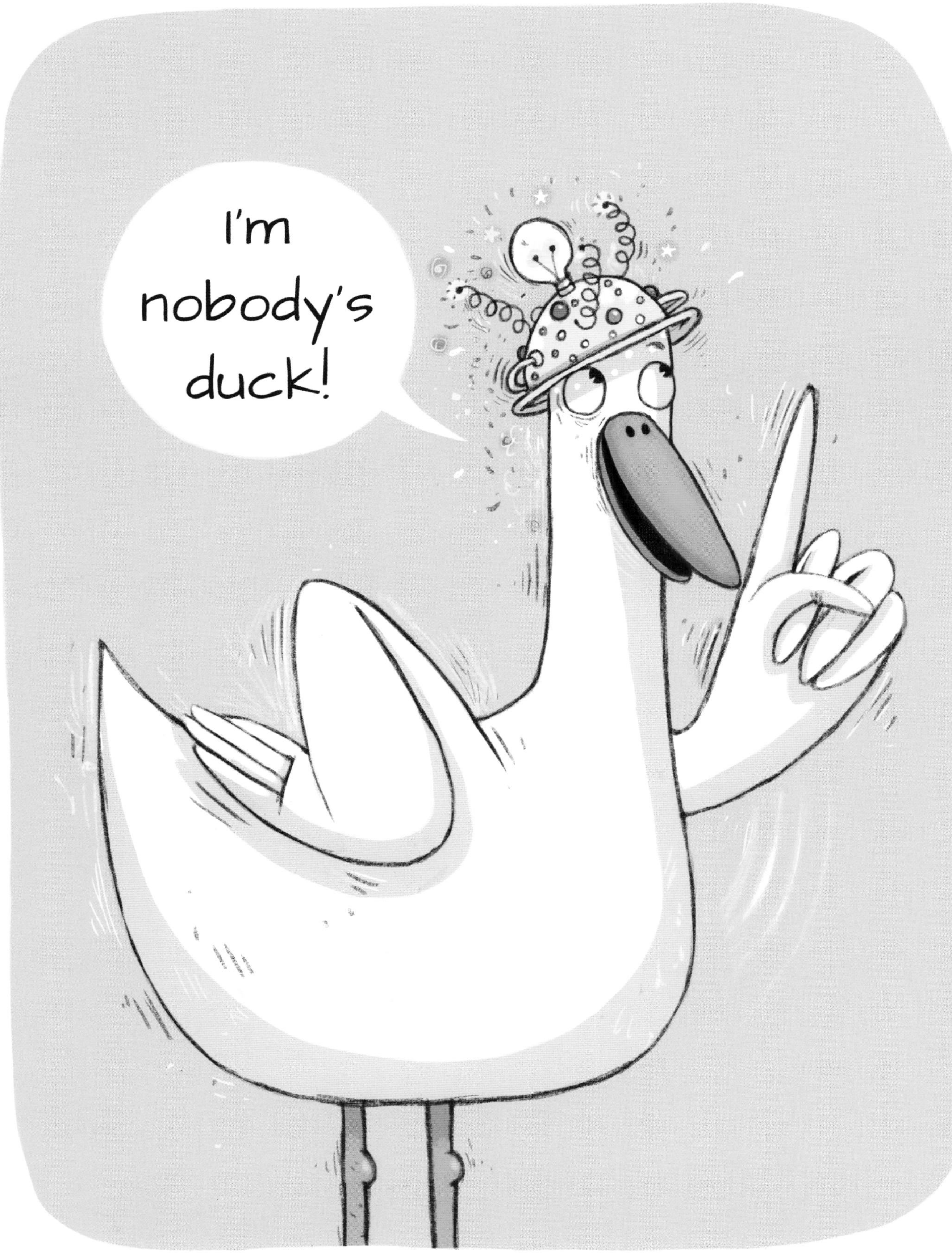
I'm nobody's duck!

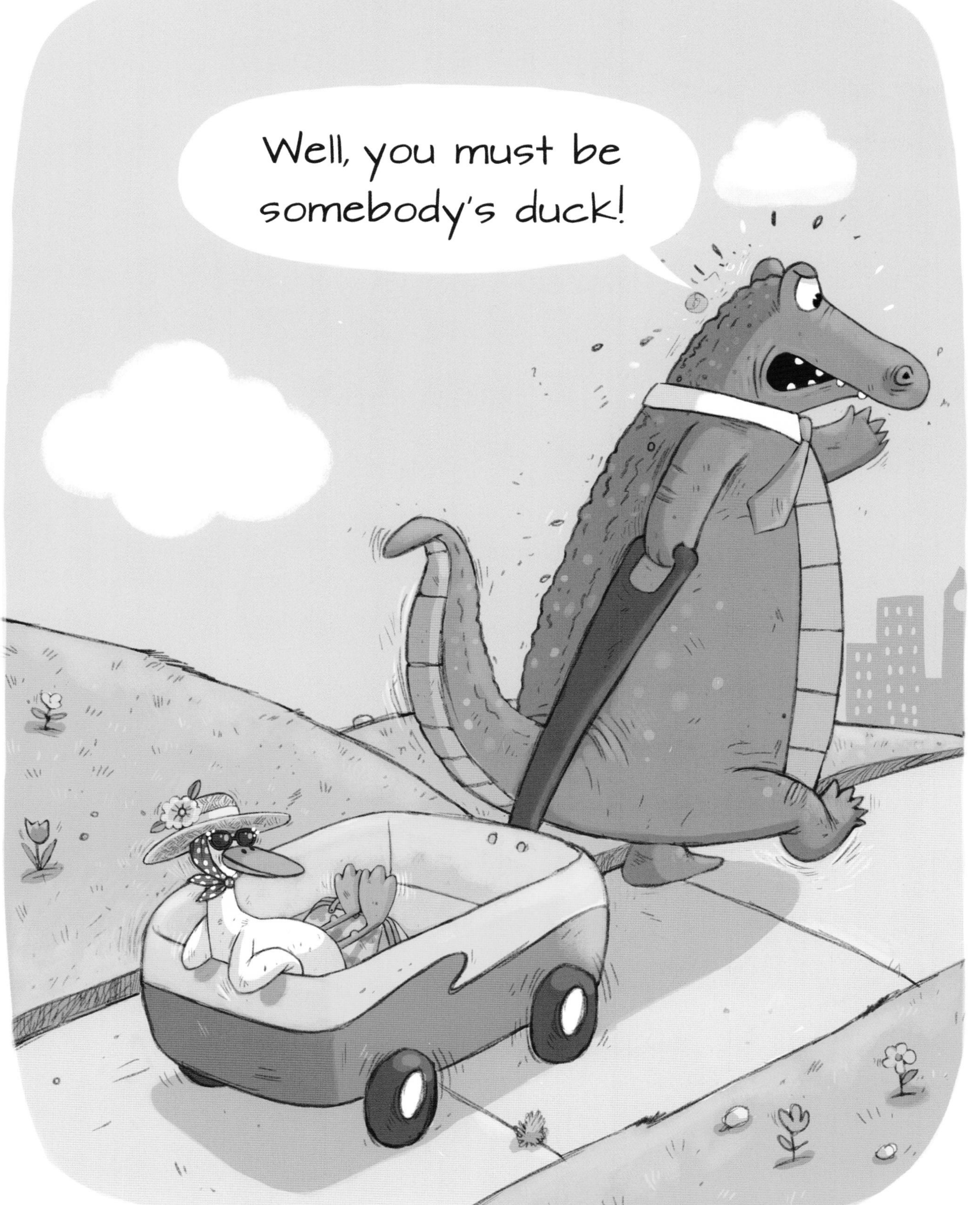
Well, you must be somebody's duck!

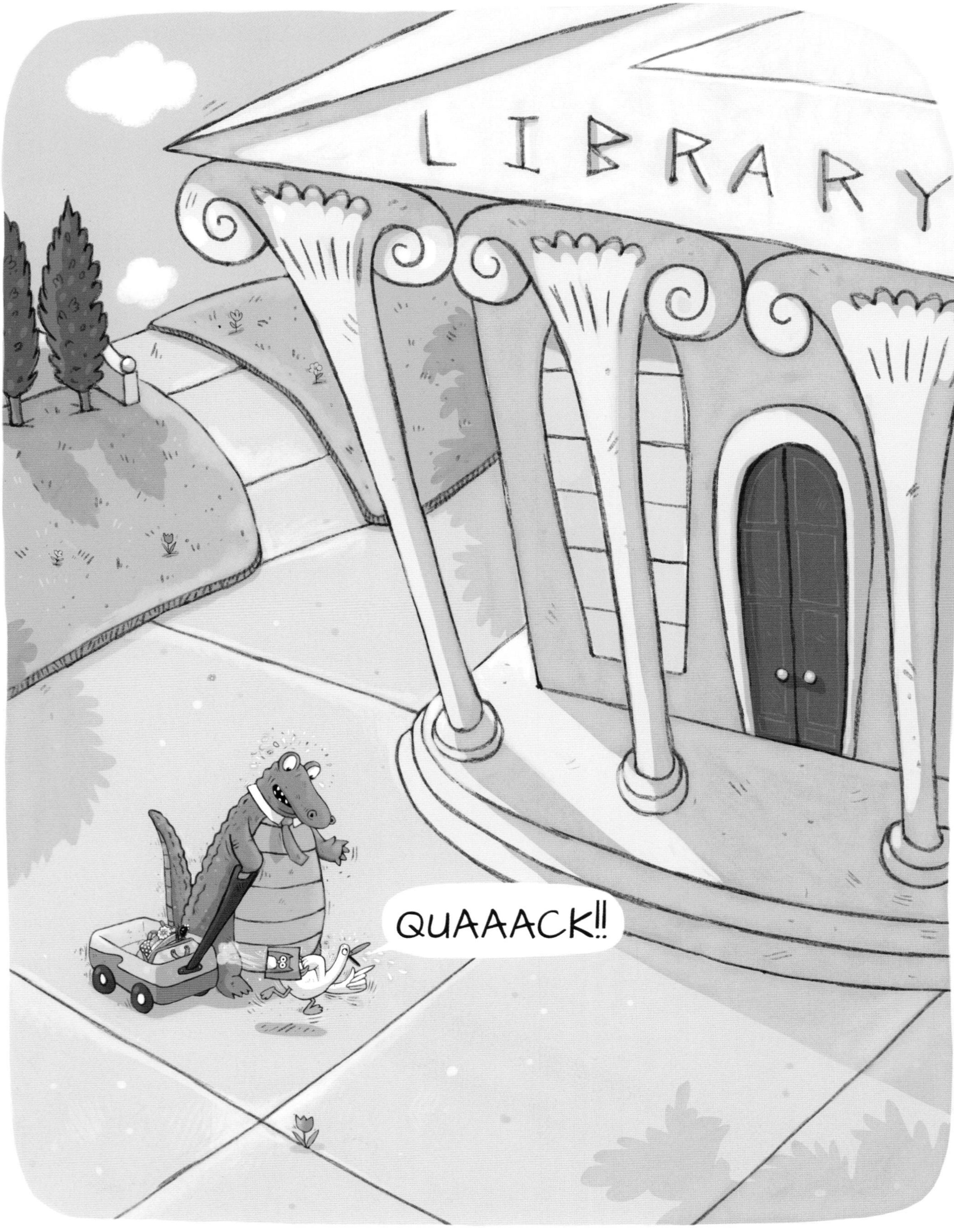
LIBRARY
QUAAACK!!

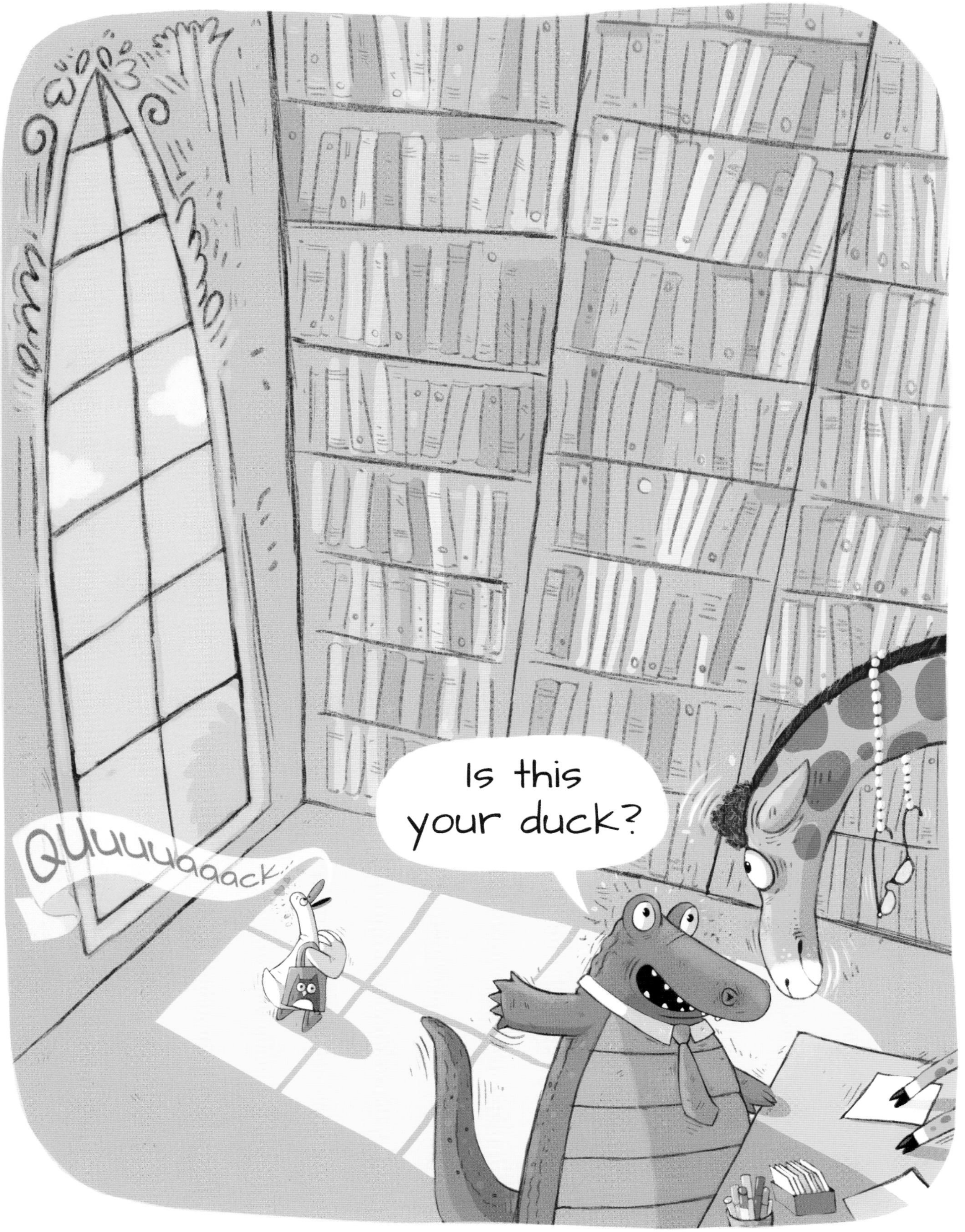
Quuuuaaack!
Is this your duck?

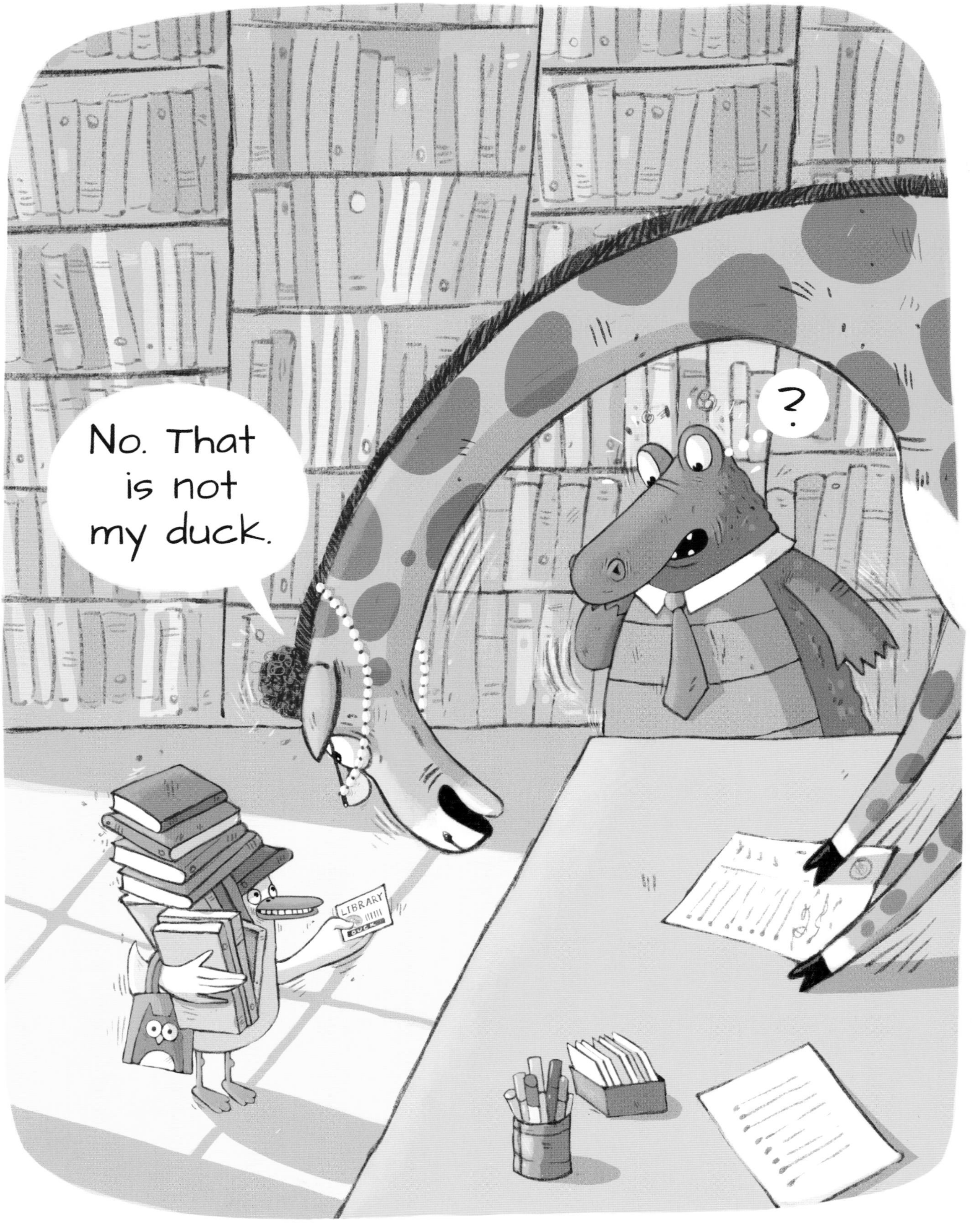
No. That is not my duck.
?
LIBRARY
DUCK

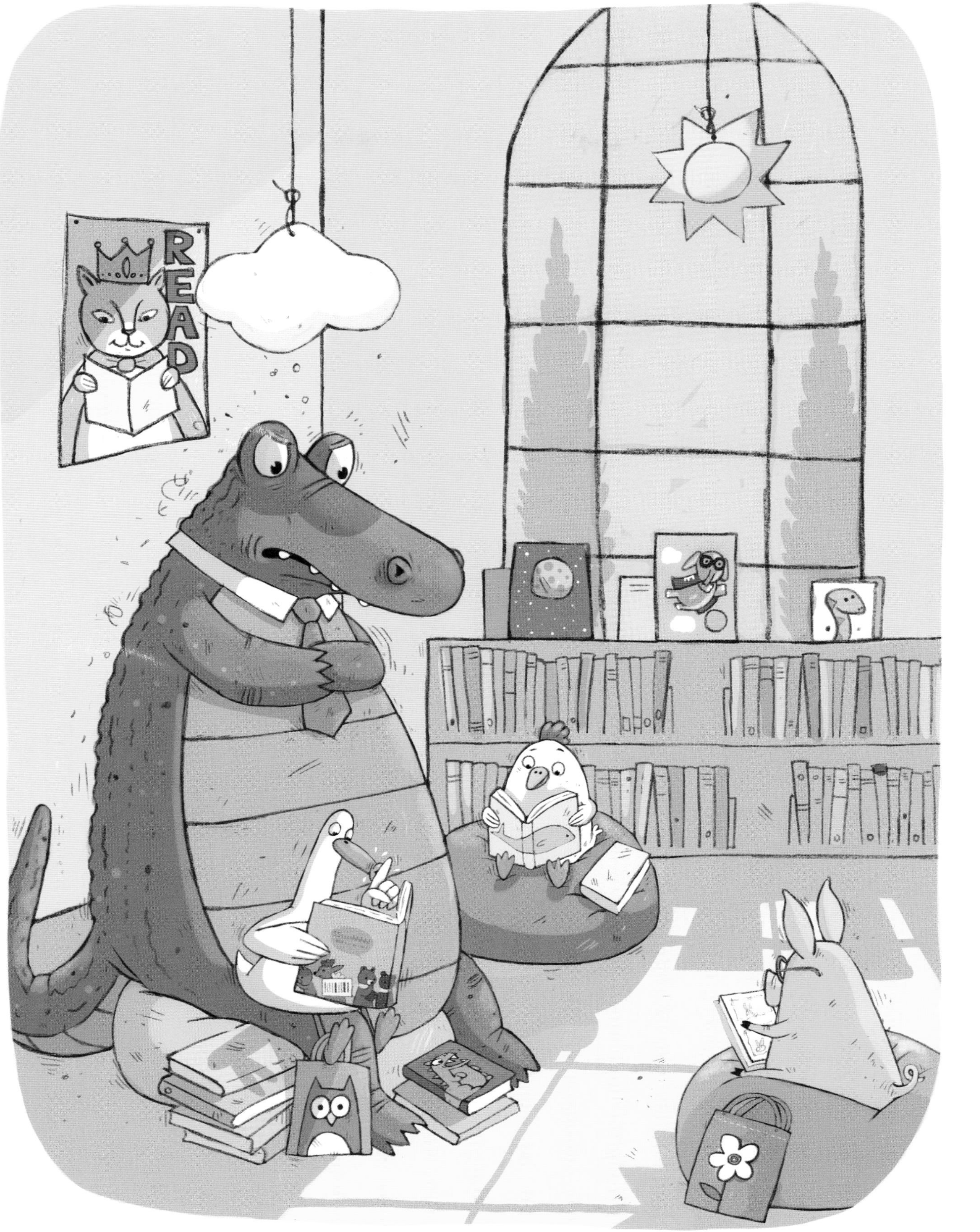
READ

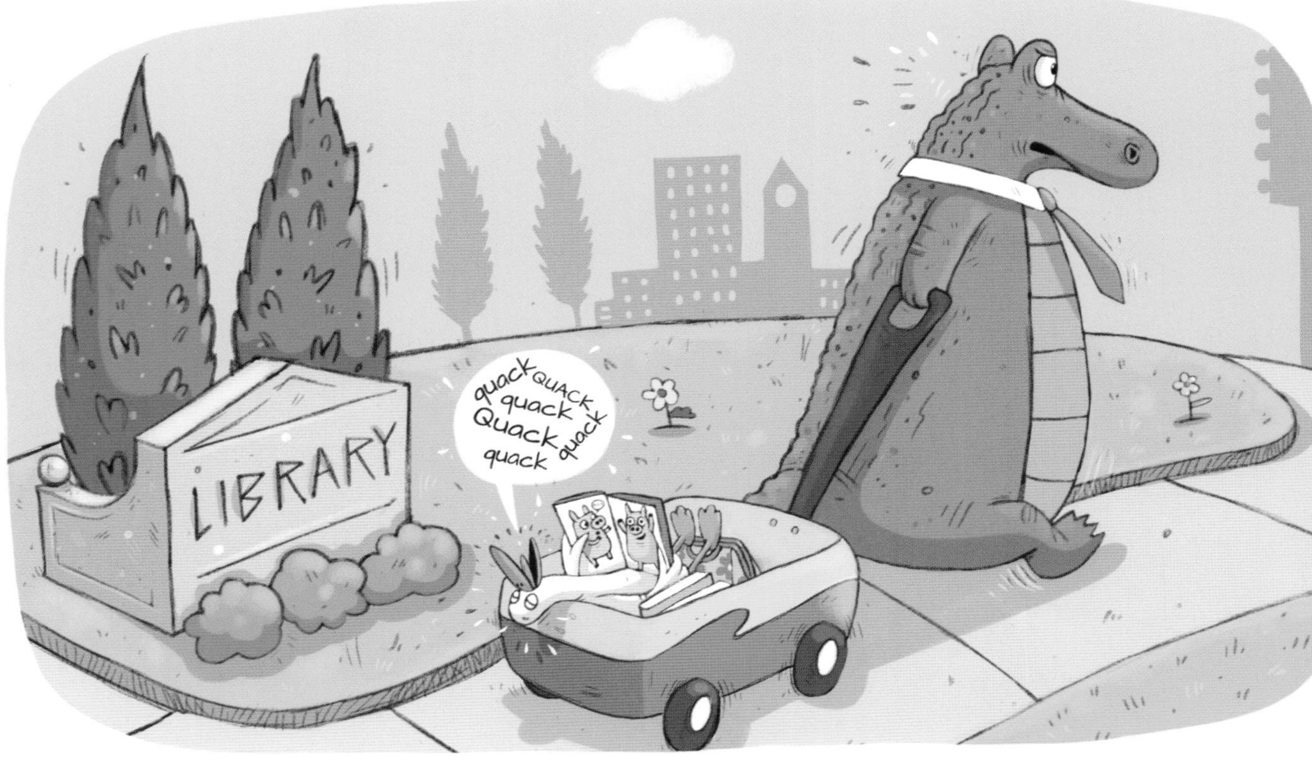
LIBRARY
quack QUACK quack Quack quack quack

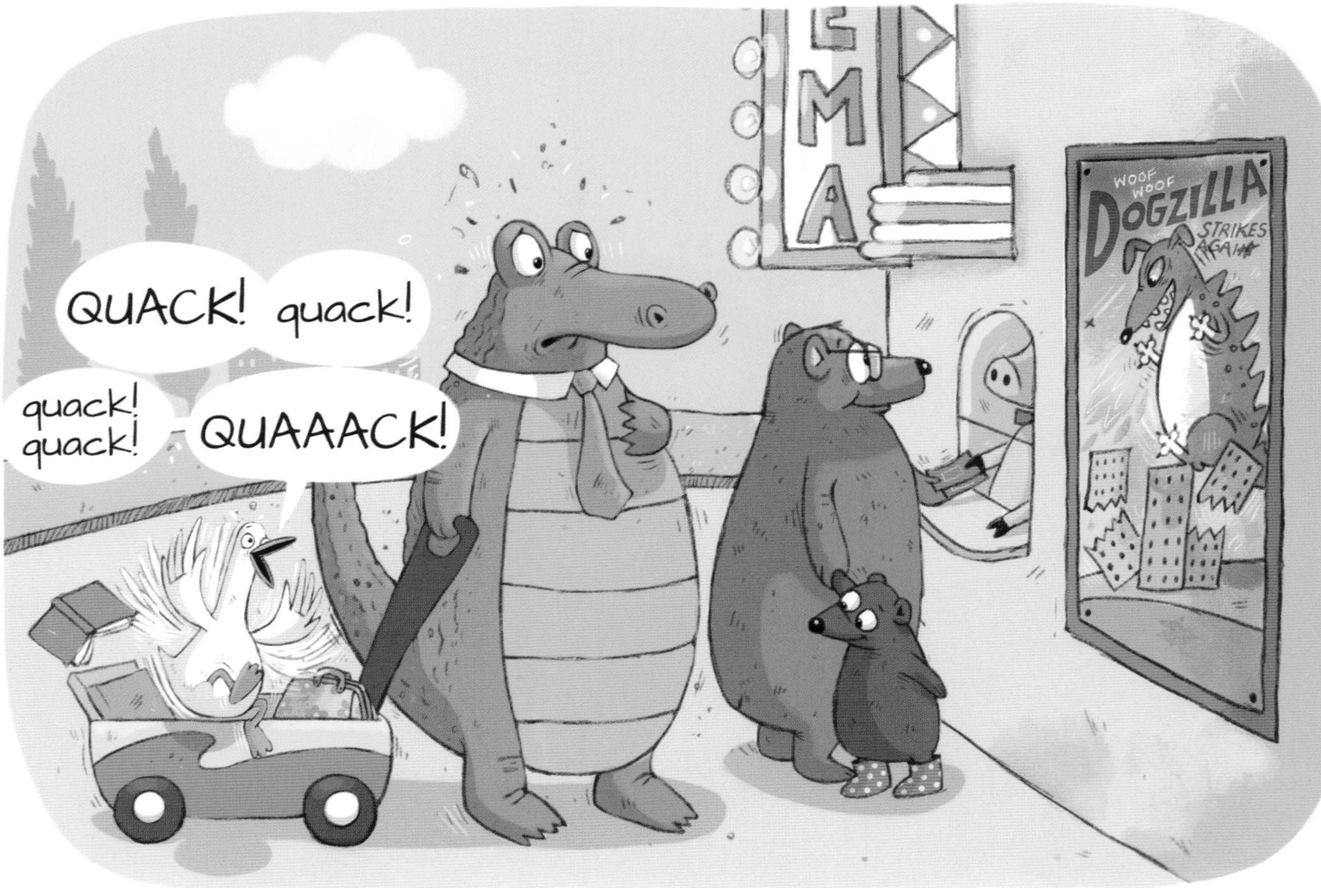
WOOF WOOF DOGZILLA STRIKES AGAIN
QUACK! quack!
quack! quack!
QUAAACK!

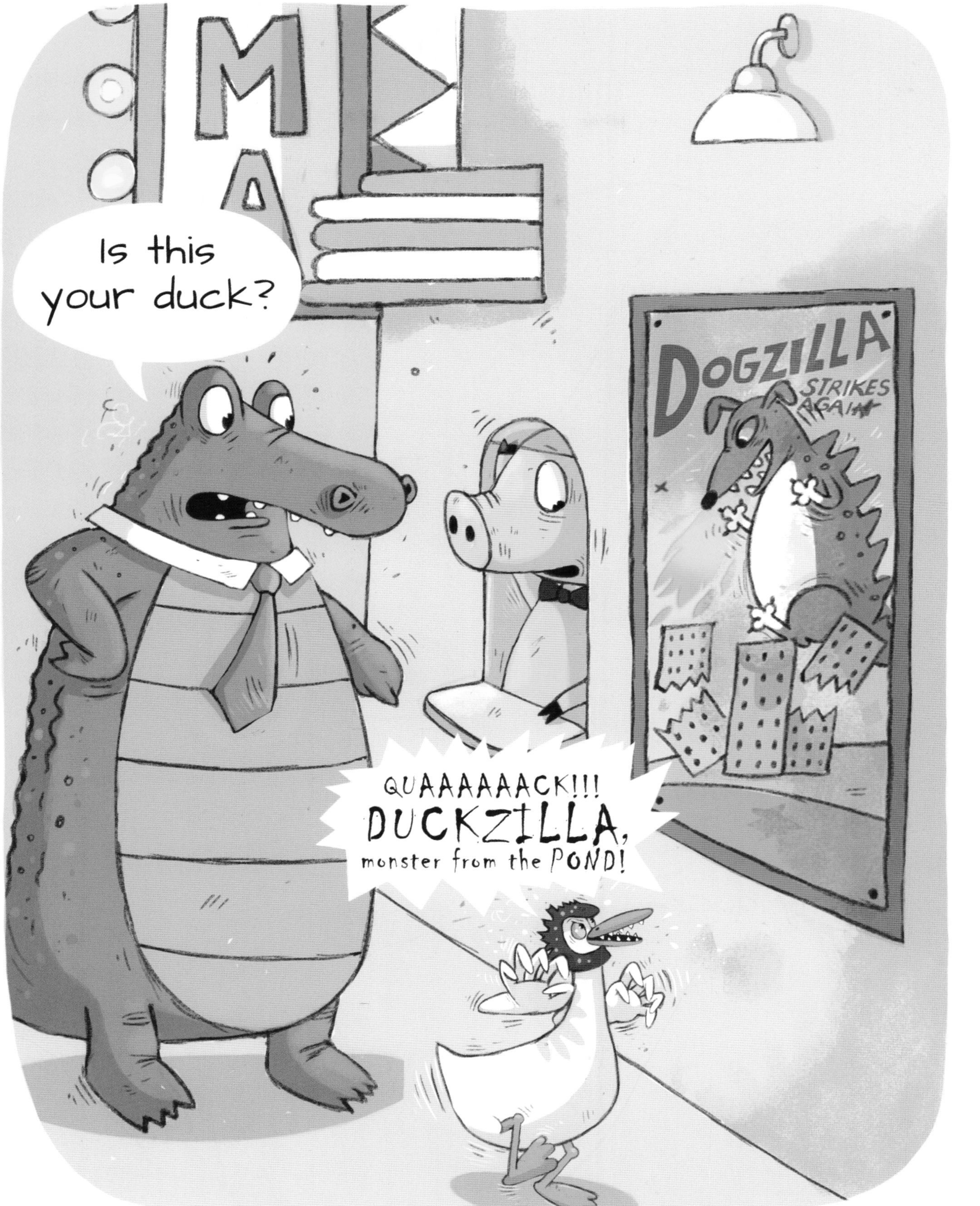
Is this your duck?
DOGZILLA STRIKES AGAIN
QUAAAAAACK!!! DUCKZILLA, monster from the POND!

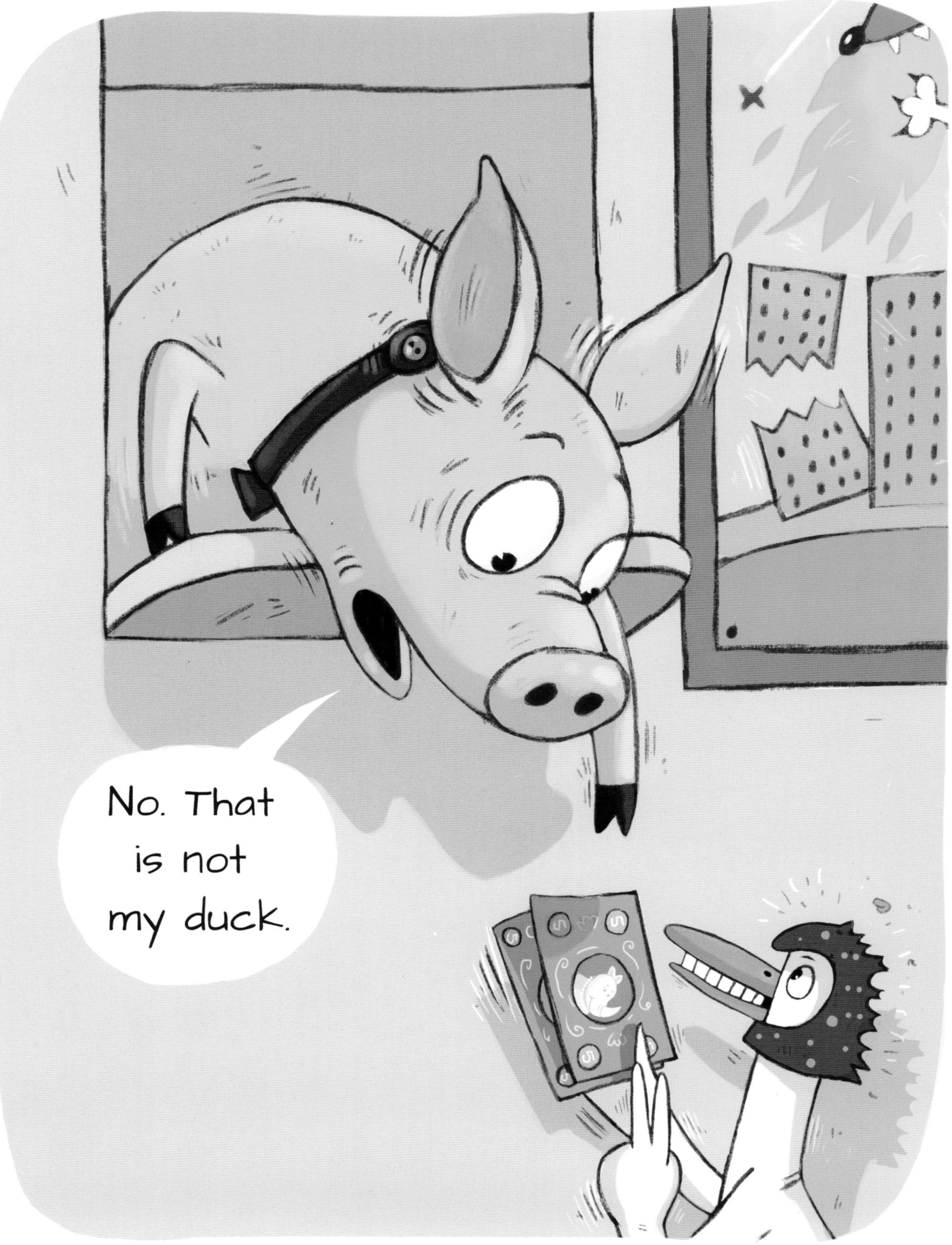
No. That is not my duck.

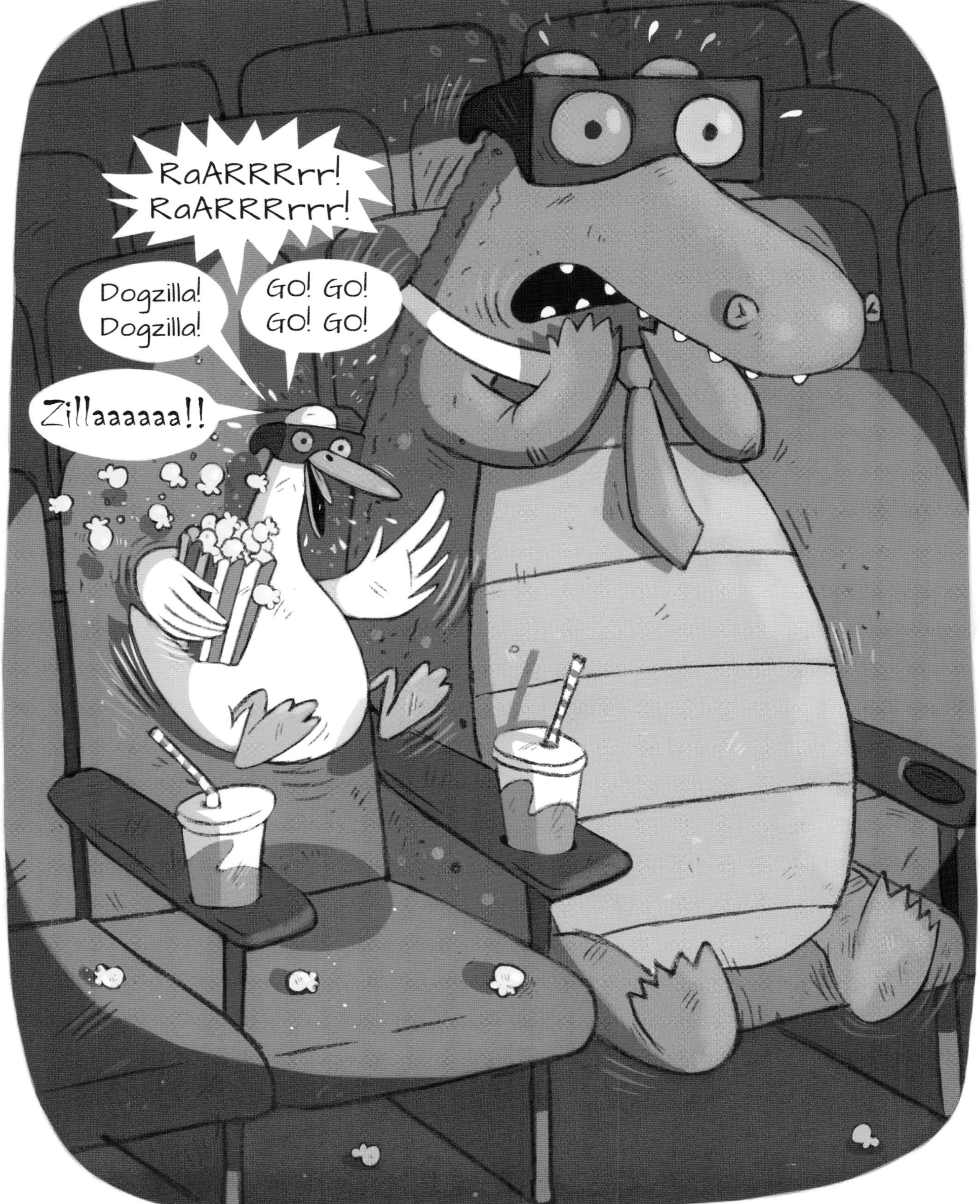
RaARRRrr!
RaARRRrrr!
Dogzilla!
Dogzilla!
GO! GO!
GO! GO!
Zillaaaaaa!!

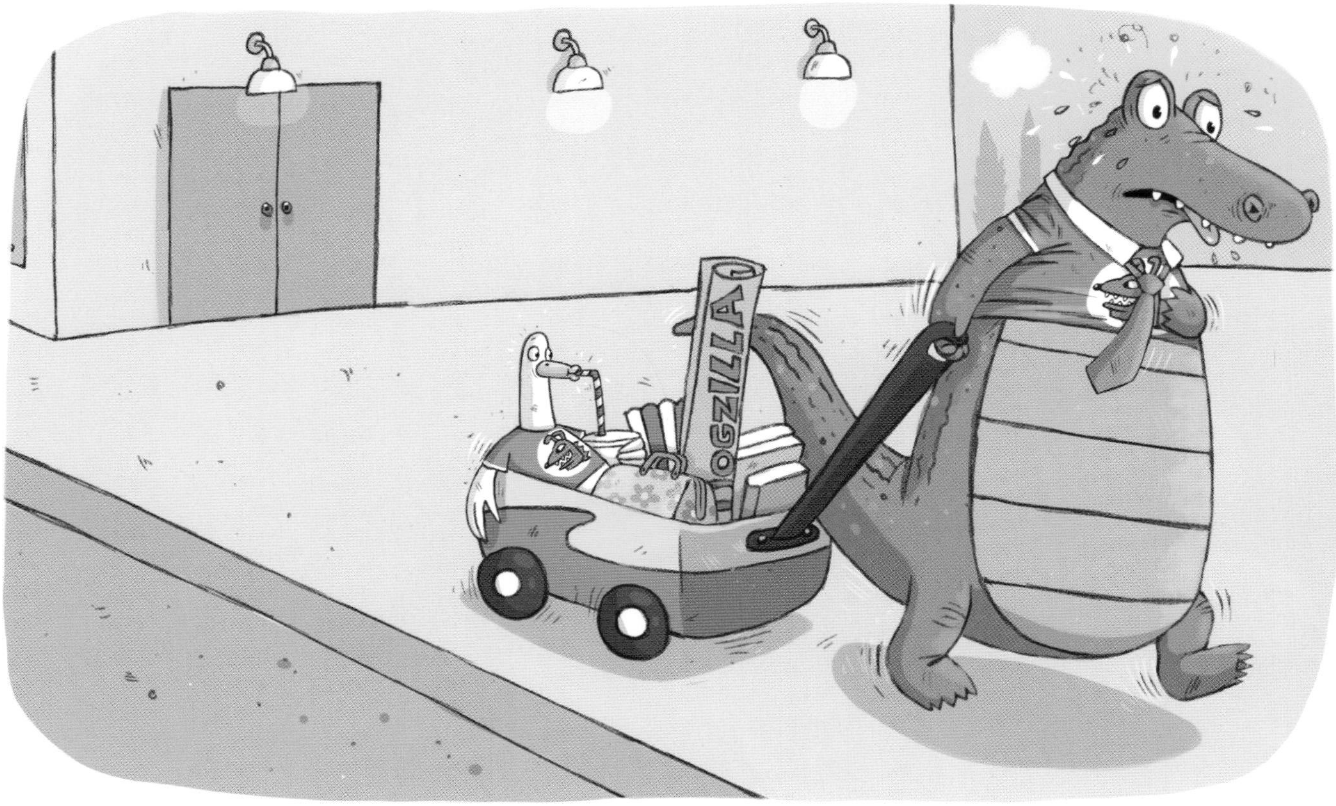

OGZILLA

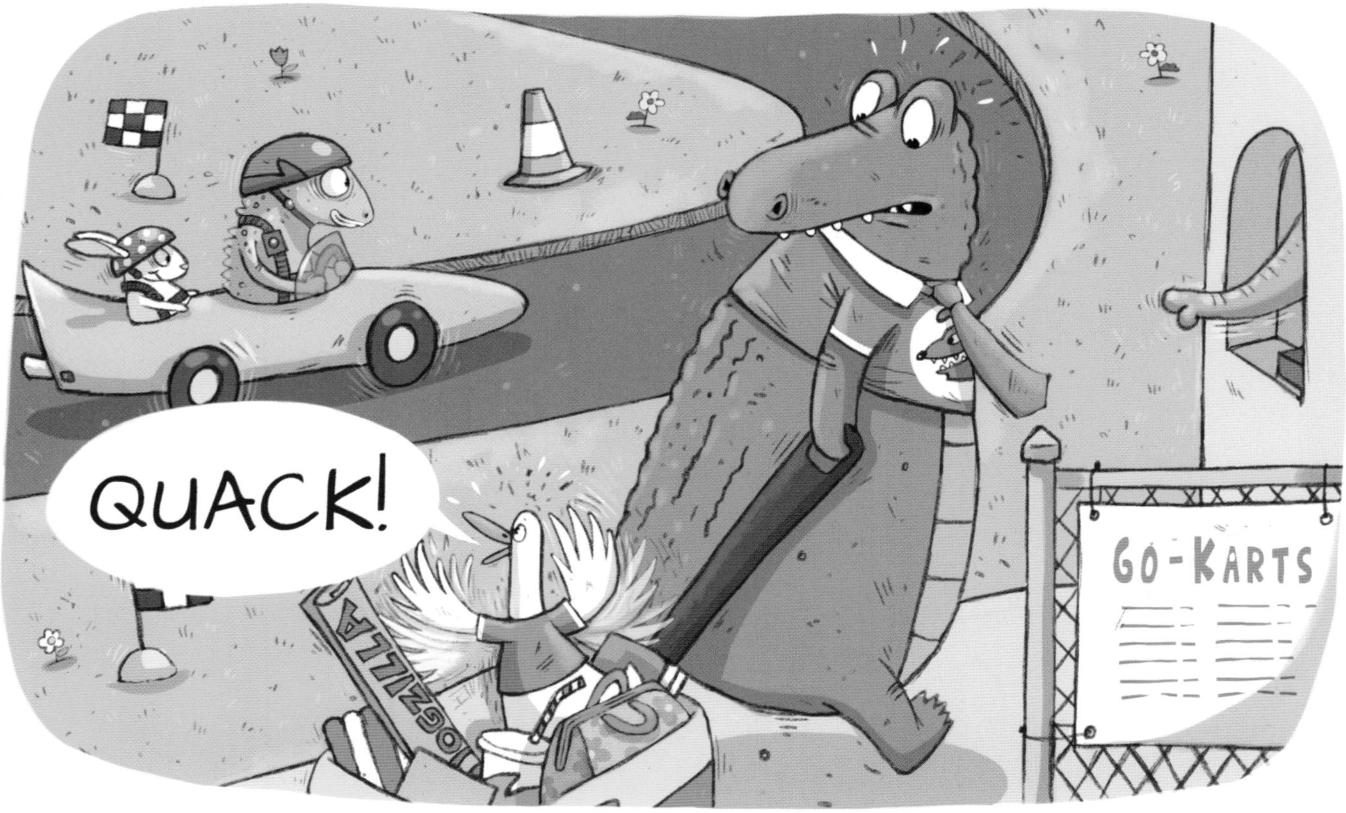

QUACK!
OGZILLA
GO-KARTS

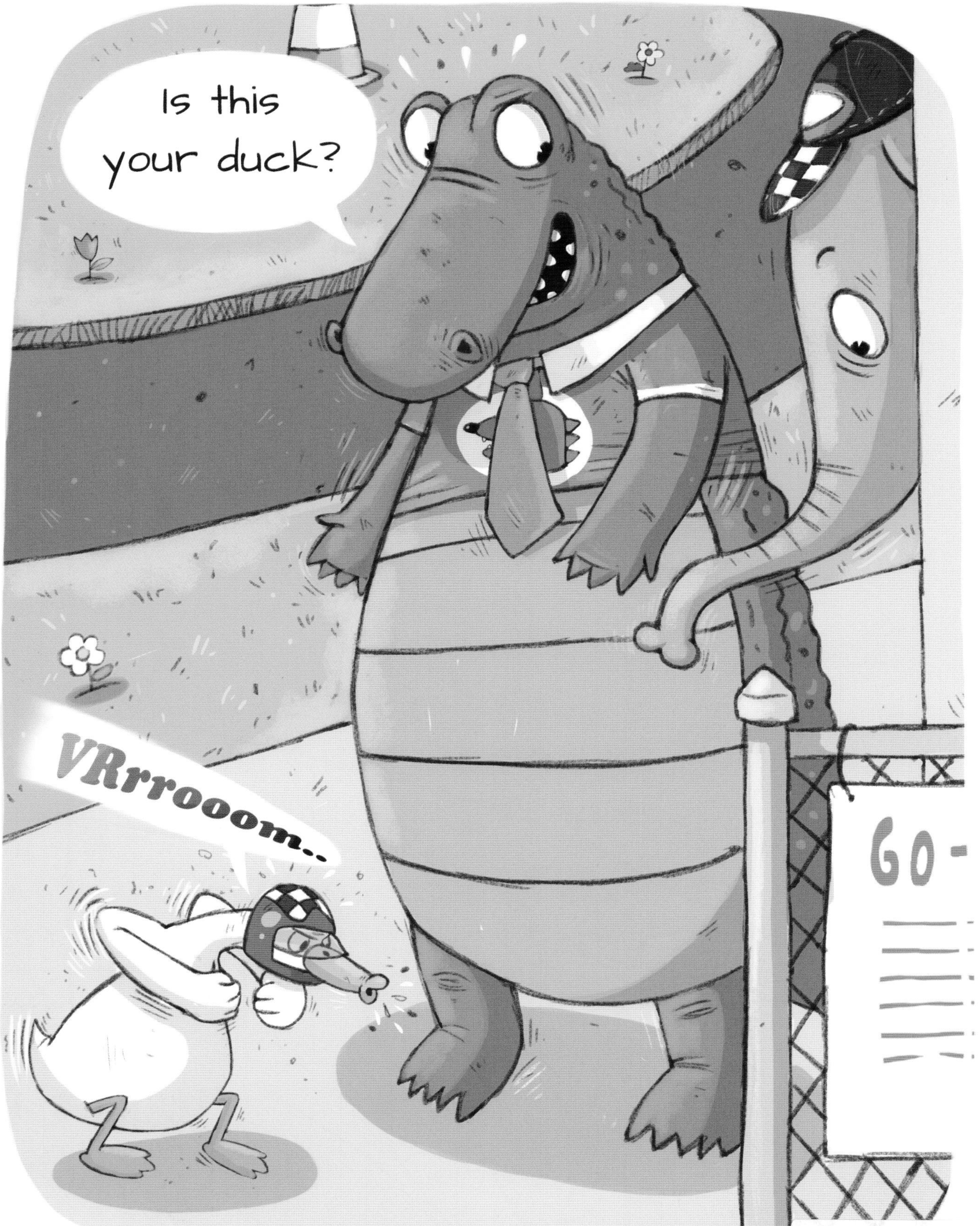
Is this your duck?
VRrrrooom...
GO-

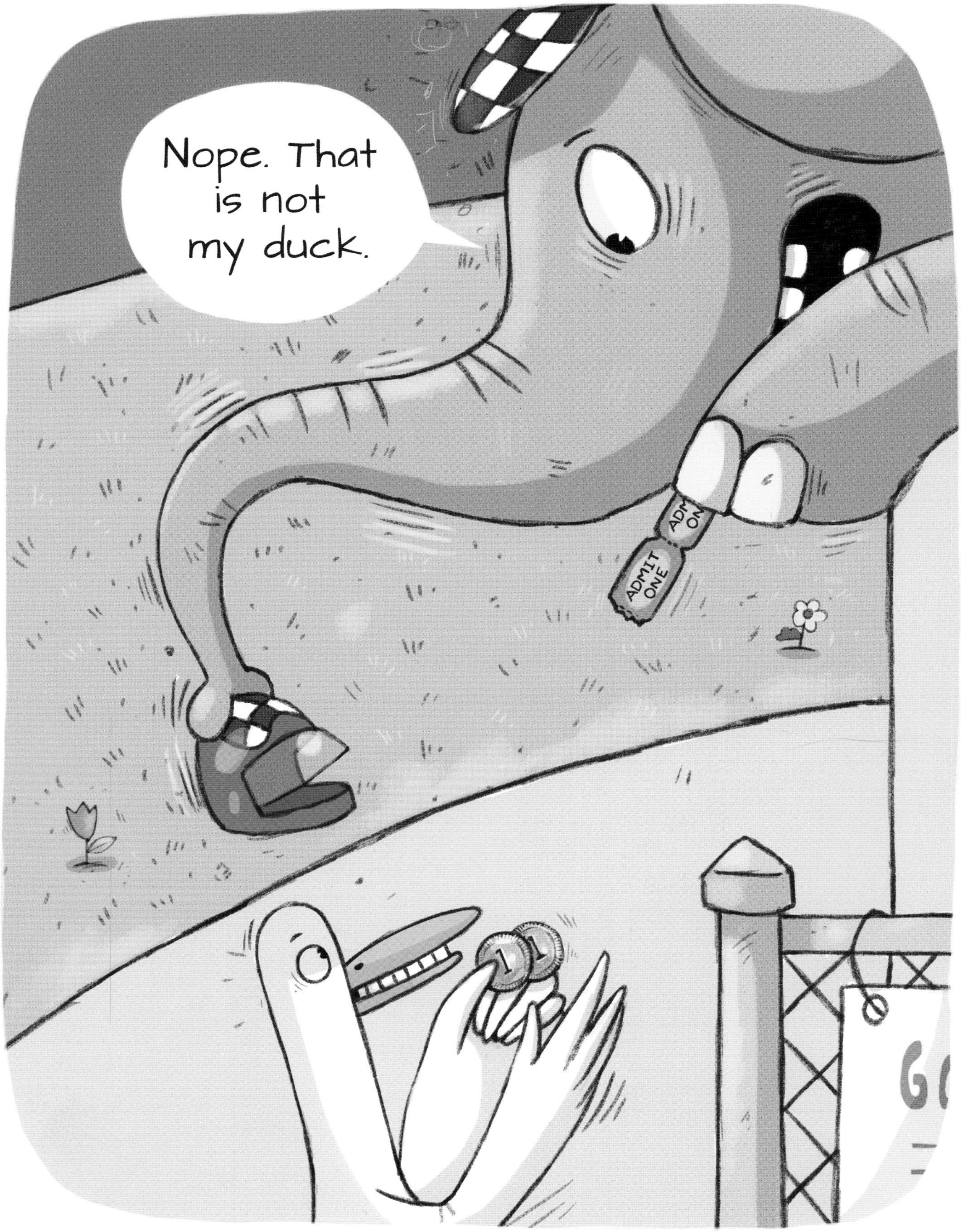
Nope. That is not my duck.
ADMIT ONE
ADMIT ONE

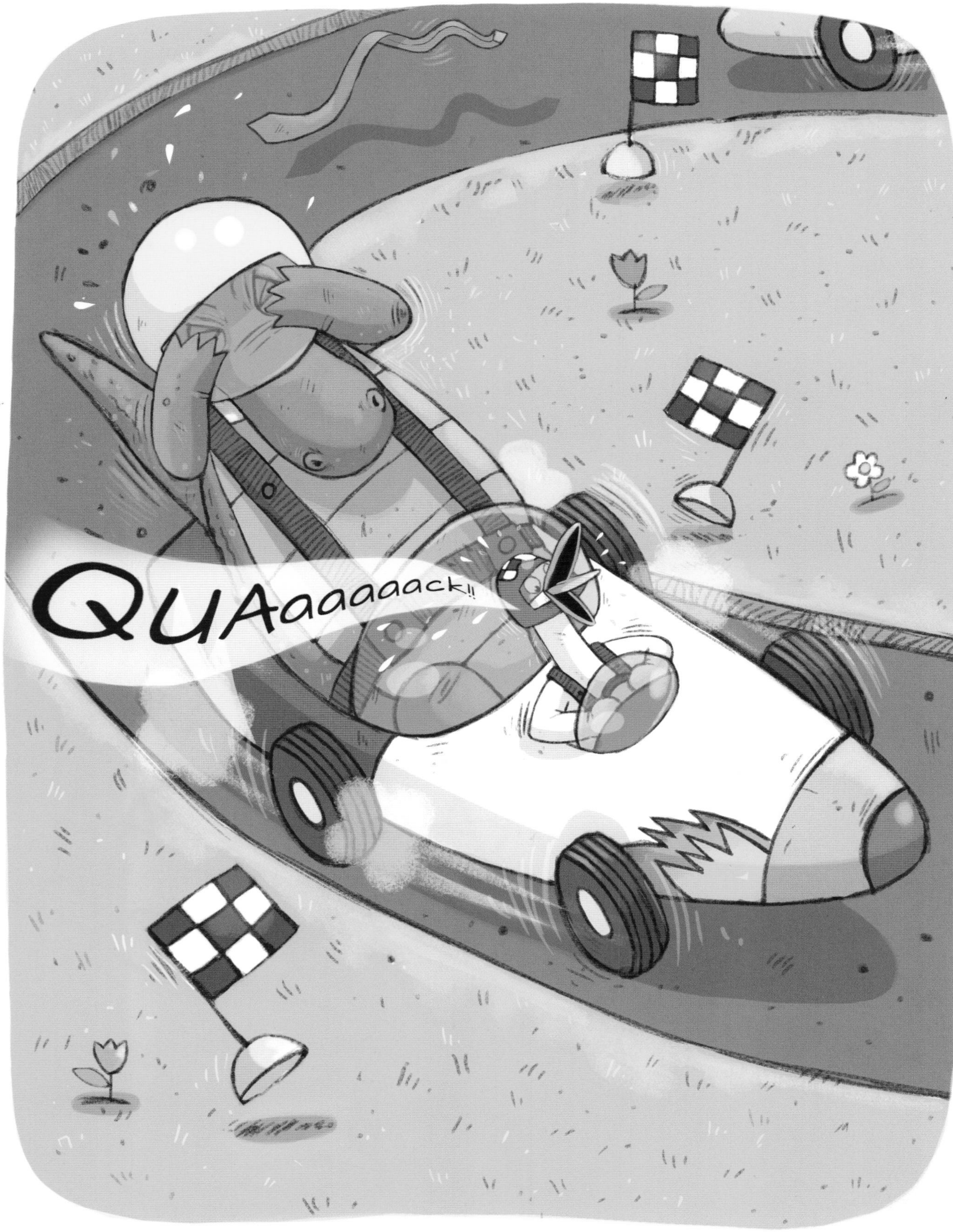
QUAaaaaack!!

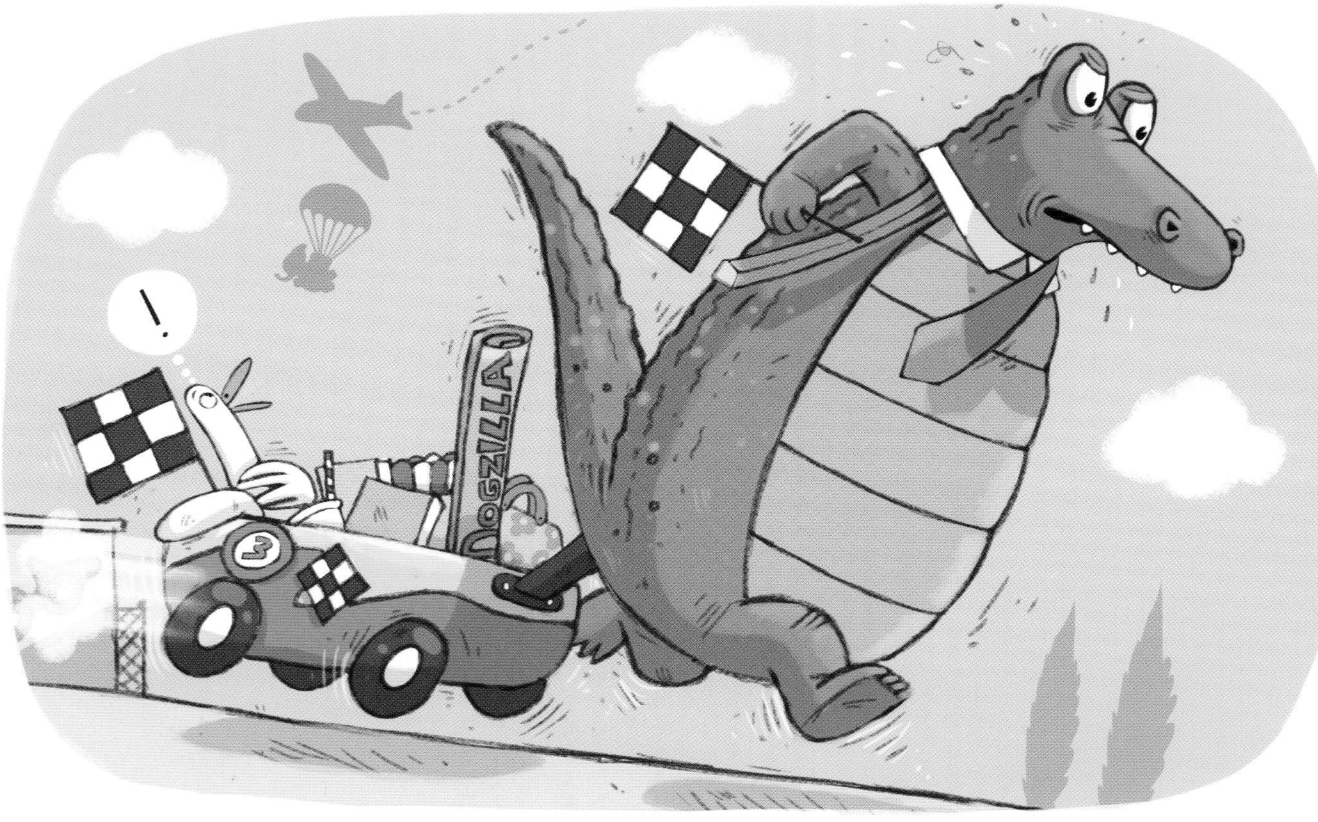
!
DOGZILLA

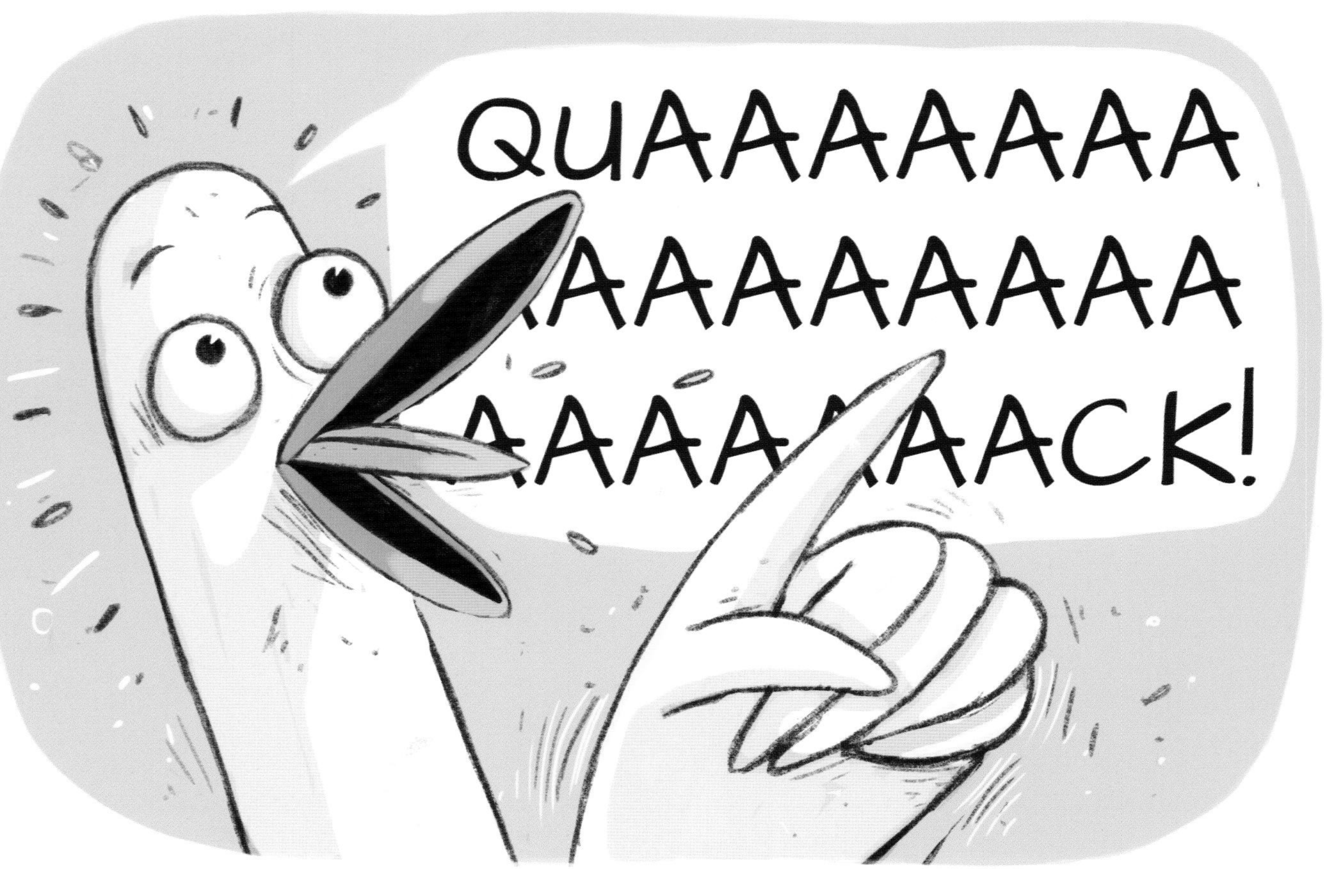
QUAAAAAAAA
AAAAAAAAA
AAAAAAACK!

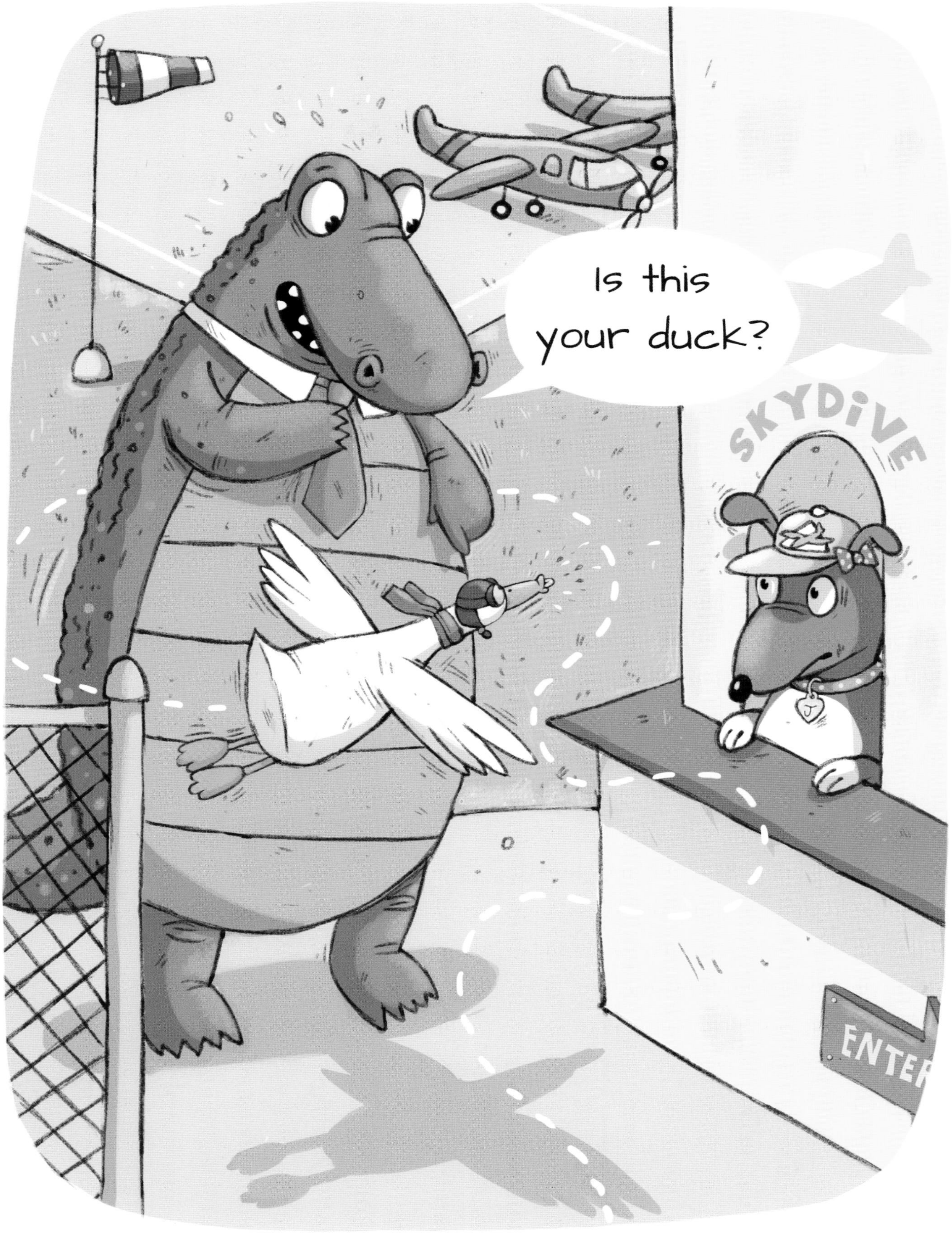
Is this
your duck?
SKYDIVE
ENTER

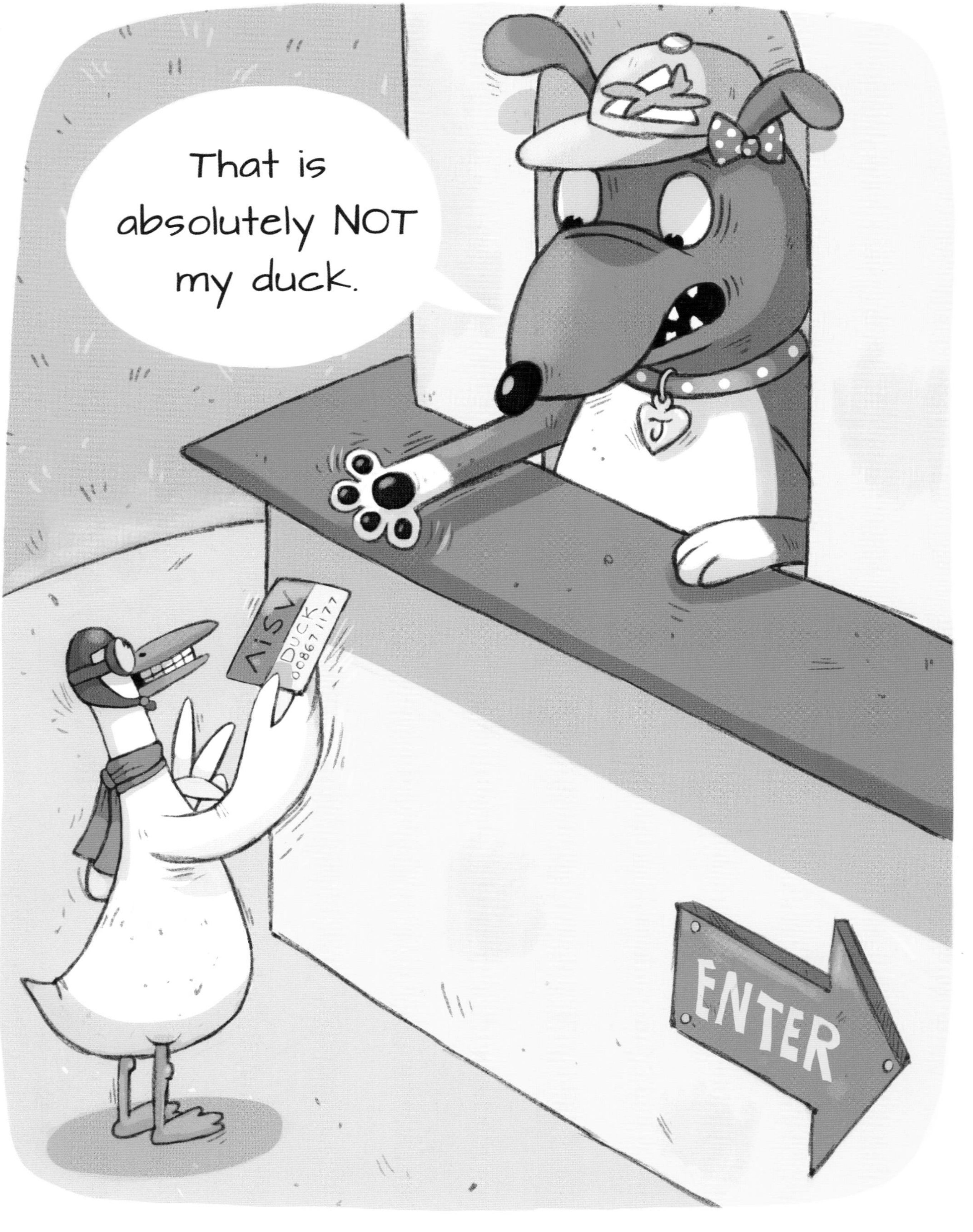
That is absolutely NOT my duck.
DUCK
ENTER

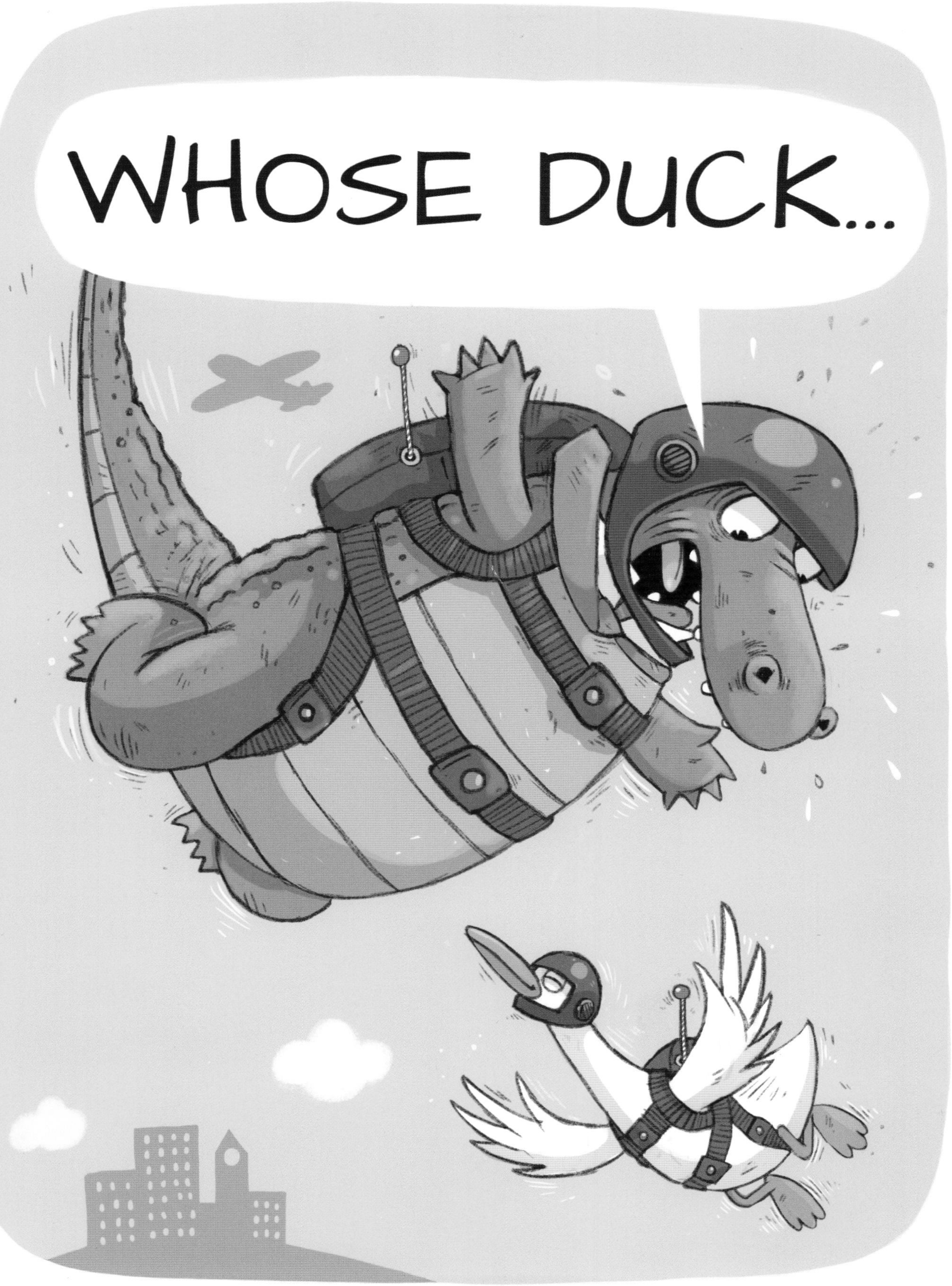
WHOSE DUCK...

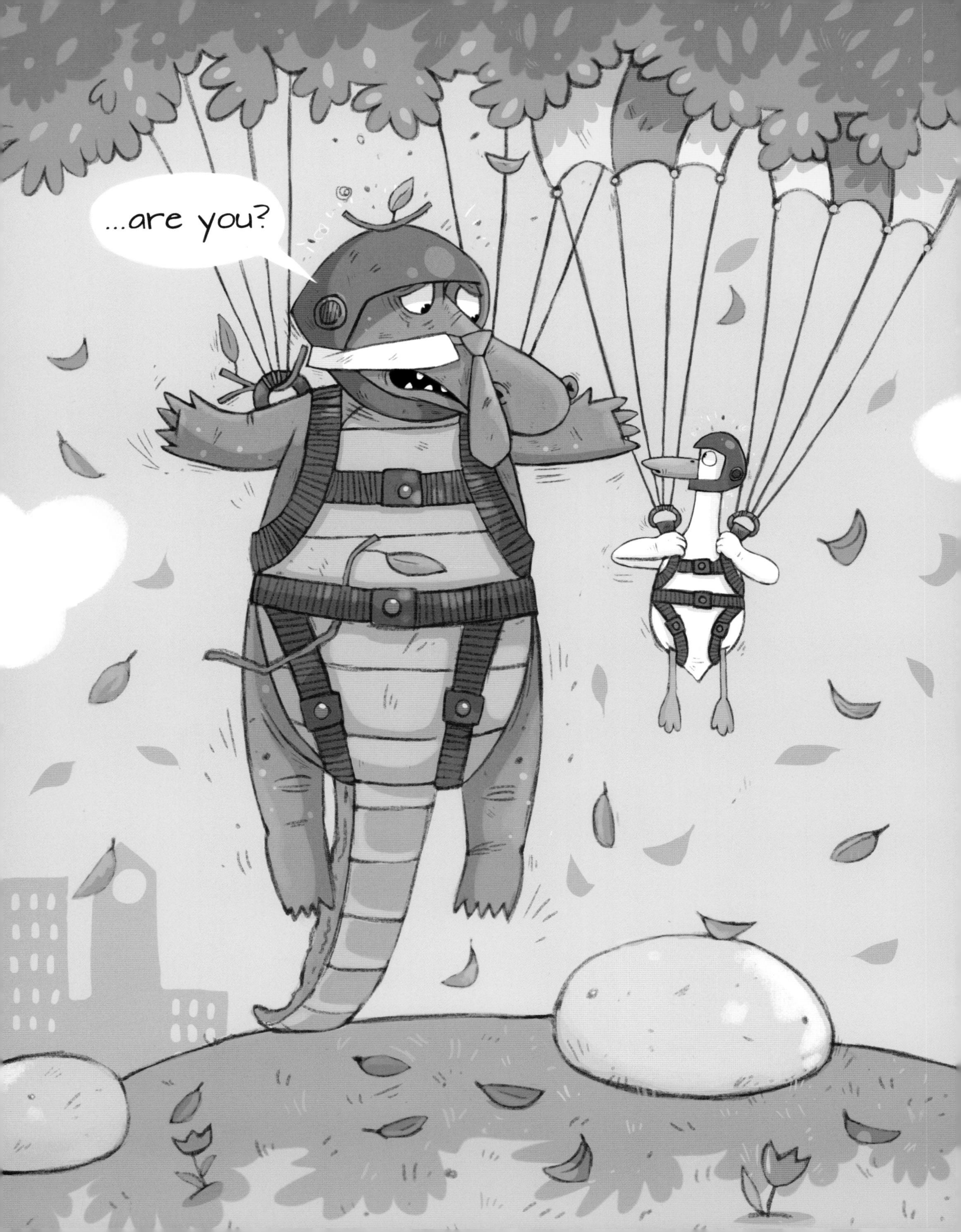
...are you?

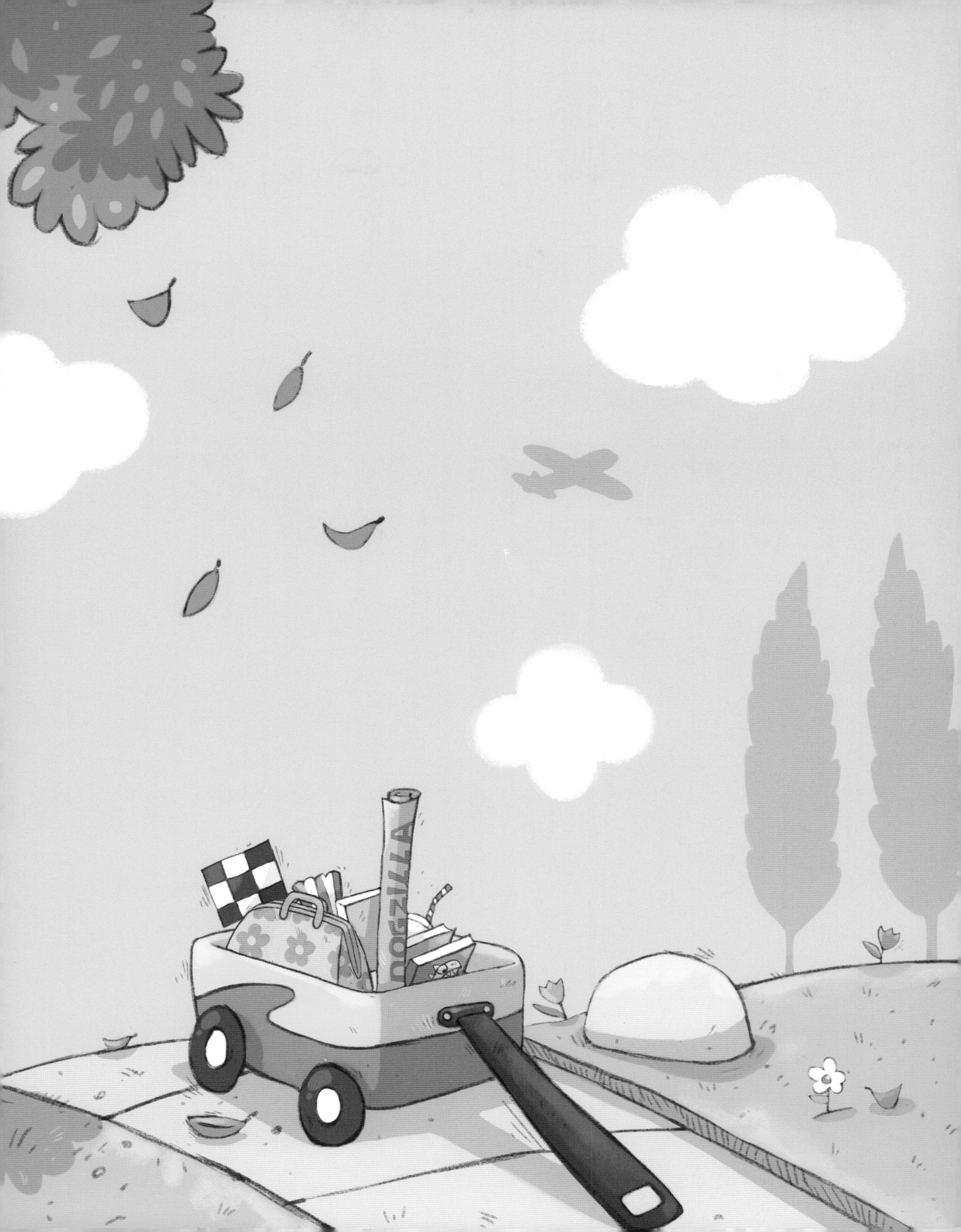
DOGZILLA

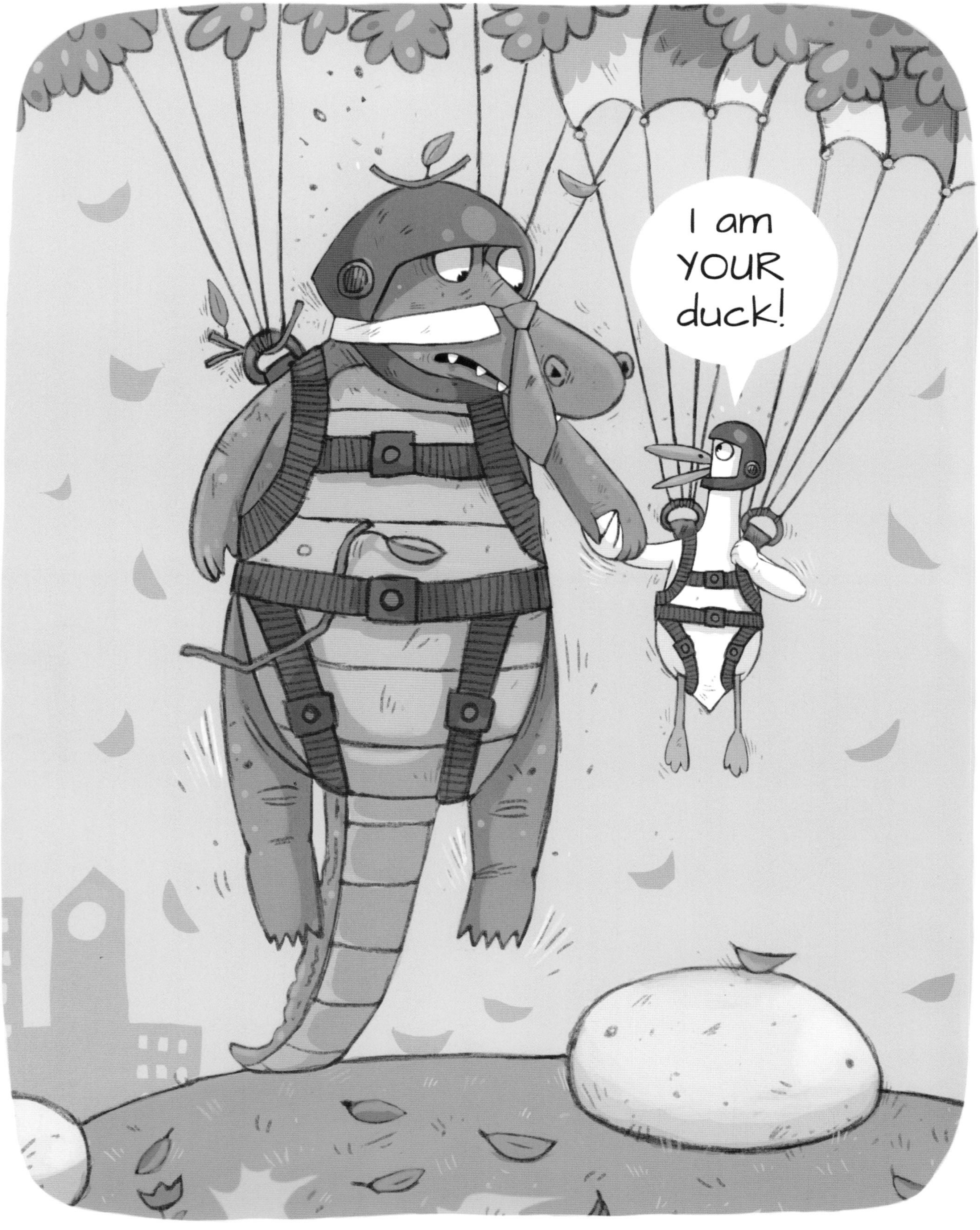
I am YOUR duck!

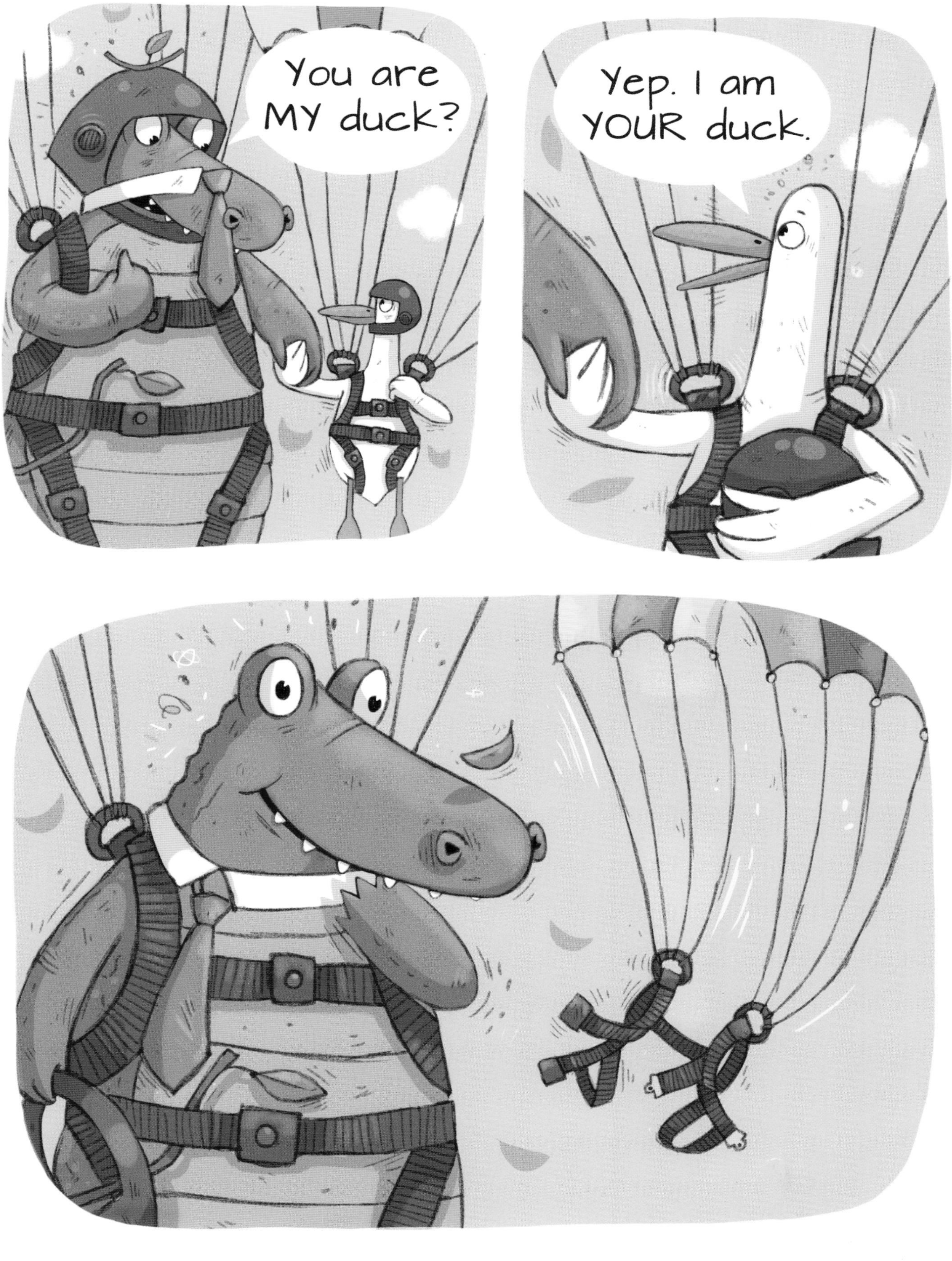
You are MY duck?
Yep. I am YOUR duck.

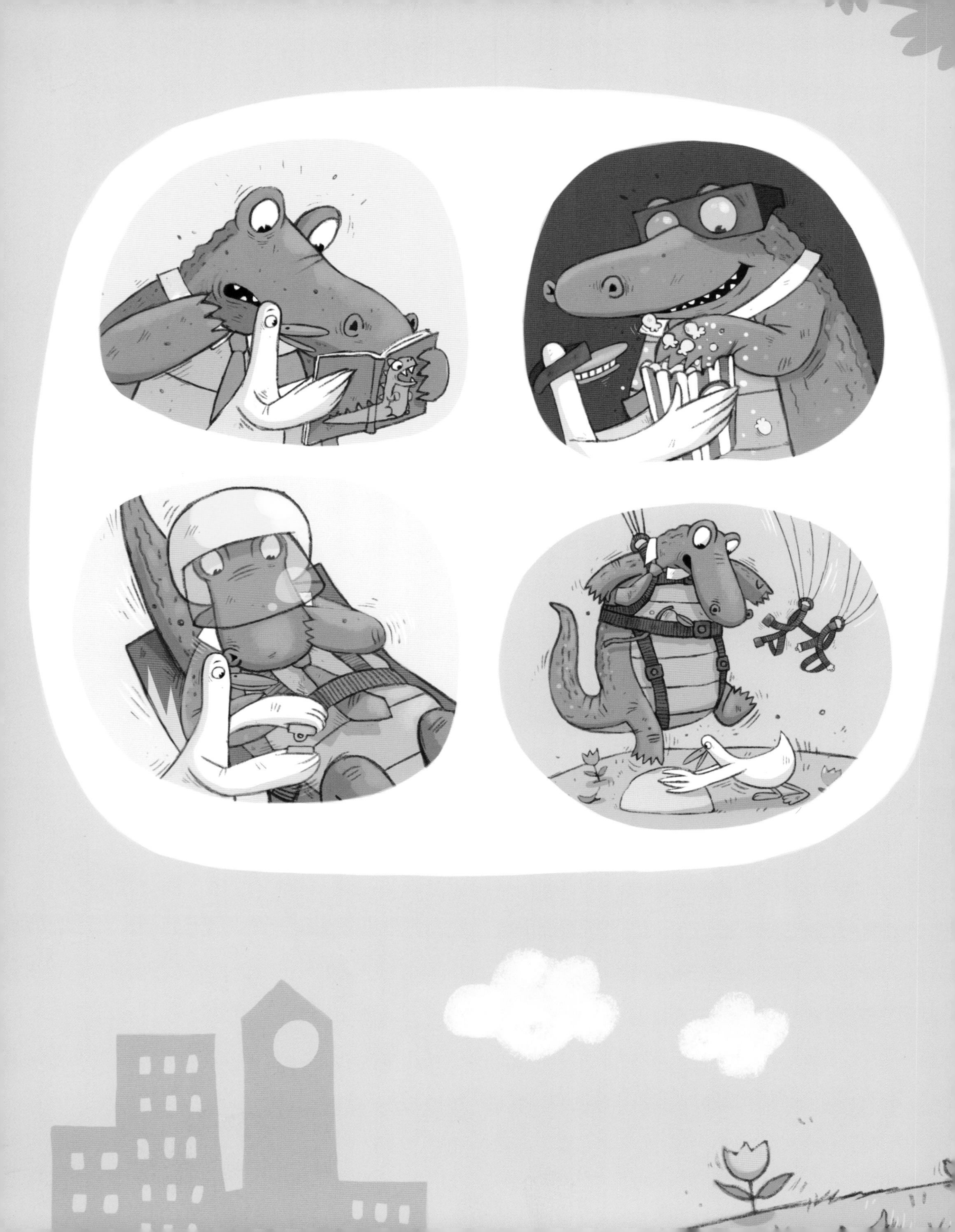

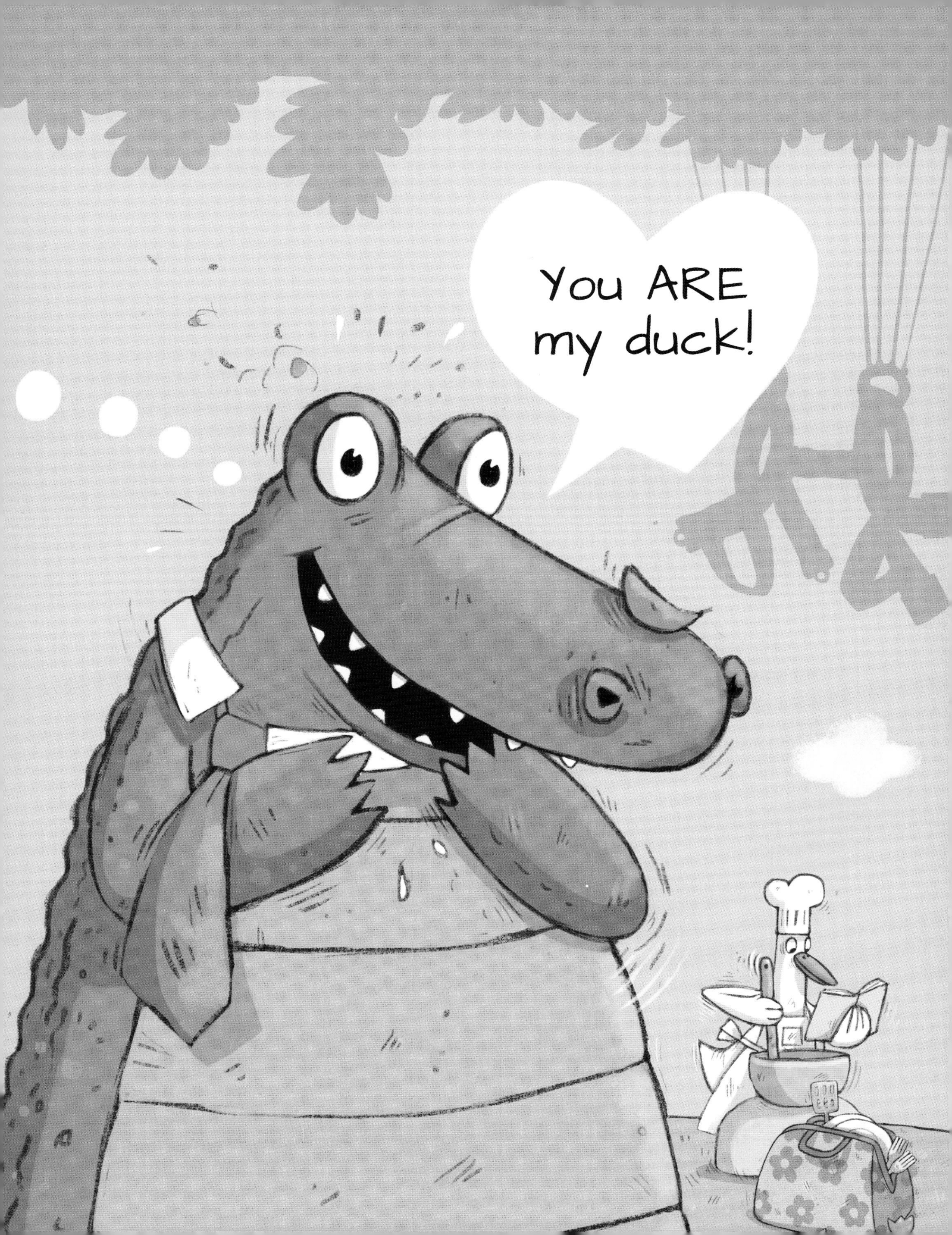
You ARE my duck!

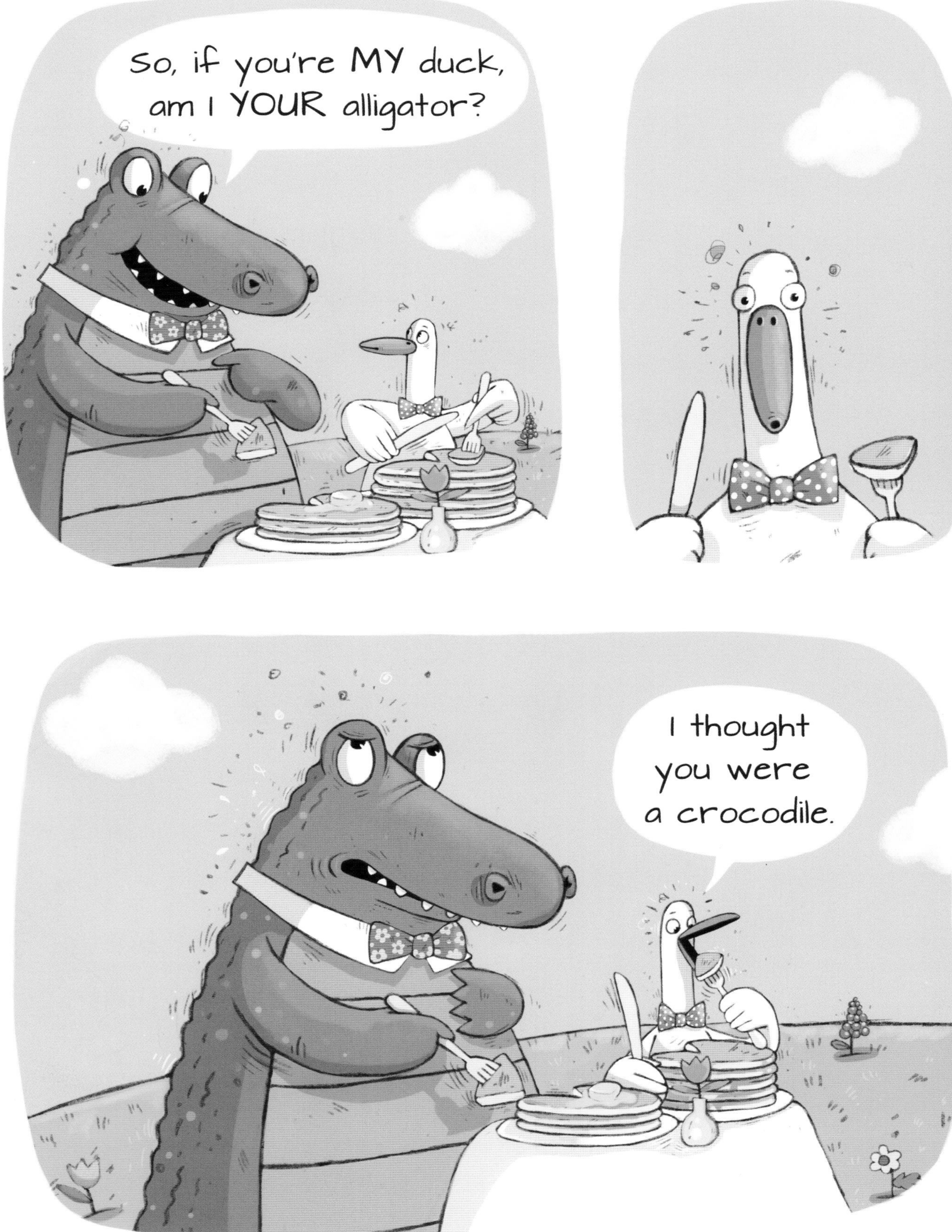
So, if you're MY duck,
am I YOUR alligator?
I thought
you were
a crocodile.